The Last Men in the North

Edward Ashton

ISBN:978-0-9930409-0-0

Dedicated to my granddaughters, Olivia and Maya.

With grateful thanks to my son, Christopher, for his critical support throughout the writing of this book.

CONTENTS

A very long time ago, two tribes of humans lived by each other in adjacent valleys. One tribe were the humans we see about us today, while the other tribe was a sub-group of the Neanderthals known as the Denisovans. It has recently been discovered that some Eurasians have 1-4% of Neanderthal genomes. So, if you look very closely at those who you pass in the street, you may just see one or two who have these ancient humans in their ancestry. The Last Men in the North is a story that shows how these ancestors of ours learned from each other, sometimes killed one another, and occasionally grew to love and care for each other.

MELTING SNOW

Doctor Alan Ramsay was once more flying over Siberian mountain ranges and now knew for certain that not only did he not enjoy flying in helicopters, he especially hated flying in old Russian helicopters. He had spent the last month in their dilapidated cabins that invariably reeked of kerosene, while being shaken to pieces, deafened and frozen. Just for once, why could he not get to ride in a modern American or French chopper? This ancient Mi-8 had probably spent its early years ferrying Russian troops around Afghanistan. It did not help his confidence that the pilot and co-pilot were still in the hotel bar, throwing back vodkas, when he had finally staggered off to bed at two o'clock in the morning.

Not for the first time, he wished that he worked for a large and prestigious east-coast university and not the small mid-western one where he was a climatologist in the Department of Geography. Unlike wealthy universities, that sent large well resourced expeditions to camp on the Greenland ice-sheet for the summer, and whose staff abseiled into crevasses and carried out other glamorous research projects, Ramsay's university did not have such resources. The consequence was that he found himself alone here in the northern Urals. He was here to study snowfall depths, tedious work at best. He was eking out his small research grant by hitching lifts wherever he could find them, which was how he found himself on this flight, with a 'world famous' snowboarder that he had never heard of. The snowboarder was flying around Siberia with a film-crew, looking for mountains with virgin runs that could be used for his next DVD release. While the film-crew were somewhat lacking in the looks department, the young snowboarder looked like an adonis, with broad shoulders, a mane of blond hair and teeth that could have been used for a toothpaste advertisement. To make matters worse, he was a great guy as well: it was hard not to feel some jealousy when you were in your fifties, out of shape and with thinning hair.

The helicopter was circling around the mountain tops, while the film-crew peered out of the finely scratched windows trying to find the perfect run for their star. Ramsay looked enviously around the cabin at the heaps of film and sound equipment that he knew would have cost more than the entire annual budget of his department. He had only one technical instrument to worry about, his ultrasonic snow depth-meter, that had been purchased second-hand from a ski school. Not heavy in itself, the batteries that it required were and completely filled a knapsack. He had spent the previous two years lugging this equipment about valleys and mountain ranges and already this year, after only a month, he was growing to hate the device. It was bad enough that he was doing this backbreaking work now, but he knew that three years' data was not enough, he would have to return here for two more years at least. His heart sank to think of it. Who knew though? From the data he had collected already, there were definite signs that the depth of snow was diminishing. When he came to publish the data, he might, just might, be requested to attend in the wood-panelled boardroom of a prestigious university and be invited to take a professorship there. It was a dream that allowed him to smile at times like this.

The only woman in the film-crew, the Director, was making her unsteady way, hand over hand, holding onto the battered seat-backs to the cockpit door, where she stood in animated conversation with the pilot. Nodding in apparent agreement, she then hurriedly returned to her seat and sat down once more with her crew, who started to gather their baggage and equipment to ready for the landing. Pulling his tattered seat-belt as tight as he could, Ramsay waited and watched as the co-pilot appeared and stood by the large cabin-door. Responding over his headphones to the orders of the pilot, he slid back the door and the cabin was instantly filled with flying snow and a freezing cold wind as the pilot held the helicopter in a hover just above the mountain top. In an impressively well drilled operation, the snowboarder and the film-crew disappeared out of the door, while one cameraman remained behind to throw out most of the baggage to the others, then returned to his seat to be taken down to bottom of the slope to take his own shots of the snowboarder's descent. Ramsay unfastened his seatbelt, stood, then hefted the heavy knapsack onto his back, lifting the bag containing the ultrasound detector he quickly made his way to the door. He leapt out to land on the snow, then bending over ran to join the film-crew gathered a little way from the landing zone. The helicopter rose then banked away, almost blowing them over with the backwash from its rotor-blades as it left the group behind in blessed silence on the mountain top.

Ramsay sought out the Director straightaway, before she became embroiled in setting up the shoot, to remind her of what they had agreed the night before. The shoot was going to take most of the day, with the snowboarder being ferried back up the mountain after each run, so Ramsay had plenty of time to make his way down to a low ridge where he would be picked up at the end of the day. Before he left he went over and shook the hand of the snowboarder and wished him luck. His ever present sense of vertigo prevented him from even peering down the precipitous slope that was going to be used for the shoot. He took a number of depth readings on the mountain top, then set off down a gentle slope to where he could see, a long way below, a cluster of rocks on a ridge that separated two valleys. He took readings every five hundred metres, recording them with a pencil and notebook. When he had first started this research project he had used laptops and tablets to record the data, but, as he soon found out, pencils always worked whatever the temperature, and they had no need of a charged battery.

Some hours later and sweating quite heavily, he reached the rocky outcrop on the low ridge. Passing between the rocks, he came to a flat area that was flanked all around by walls of rock. Sheltered as it was from the cold wind, this would be a good place to rest while he waited for the helicopter to pick him up, so removing and dropping the knapsack of batteries and putting the scanner-bag down, he sat with his back against one of the larger rocks and looked around. None of his academic colleagues, and only a very few of his friends, knew of his one remaining guilty pleasure; he smoked. Now was the perfect time, scrabbling in his pockets he pulled out his brass lighter and a packet of cigarettes. He took his time, enjoying the pleasure that came from removing the cellophane wrapper and then the sliding out of the cigarette to be placed between his lips. He paused, enjoying the moment, then struck the lighter wheel and brought the flame up to light the end of the cigarette. Inhaling deeply, he looked up at the cold blue sky, then while breathing out the smoke in a long slow exhale he brought his gaze down to scan the geology of this strange place. The side of the rocky enclosure facing east was banked high with snow but, at about the height of a man, he could see a round dark shape that caught his attention. Despite his curiosity, he finished his cigarette first before moving. It would have felt wrong to have thrown the cigarette-end down in this pristine place, so first he nipped it out and placed it in his pocket, then stood and walked over to see what this thing might be.

It was a hole, about the size of a soccer ball, so it was quite easy to push an arm through to feel for rock, but there was no rock, only empty space. He began to pull at the sides and bottom of the hole to make it bigger, but it was hard going as the snow was so compacted. He took off his jacket, collected his breath and set to work once more, until eventually he had created a hole large enough to squeeze his body through. The bright sun illuminated what appeared to be the mouth of a cave, so ducking down he made his way tentatively inside. It was a cave, the roof too low for him to stand upright, making him bend and look about with his head tilted sideways. As his eyes became accustomed to the gloom, he saw by the distant back wall the gleam of something white. Crouching further down, he made his way to the wall where he found the skeleton of a very large creature, its head pointing towards the cave entrance. He sat down next to it, resting a hand on its broad head. As he looked about in the dim light, he could now make out that in the middle of the cave were a number of objects resting on the flat earth floor.

He gave the skull a farewell pat; then dropping forwards on all fours, he made his way across the cave floor to see what the objects could be. When he reached them he raised himself up onto his knees, lifted his lighter as high as he could then used his thumb to flick the wheel. What he saw suddenly appearing in the flickering light shocked him, a human skeleton lay there, as perfectly laid out as if on an anatomist's table.

1

THE LEAVING OF RAT

Rat sat on a rock at the head of the valley, close by the pass where his tribe would soon leave the valley to begin their long trek across the hunting-plains to head south. He was wearing his shaman's long black robe but without his ceremonial mask. Having a crippled left leg required that he had set off to these heights just after dawn, long before the rest of the tribe, and, despite the chill autumn air, had sweated heavily while limping his way up so high. He was starting to feel cold from sitting in the chill breeze that tugged at his robe. His sweat was drying on him as he regained his breath and his bony backside could feel every bump on the rock beneath him. He could see the whole tribe, climbing in a long straggling line that stretched up from the now deserted camp to where he sat. Everyone, including the older children, was bent double with heavy loads that contained food and all the supplies that they would need on the long journey ahead.

His tribe, the Salar, had lived well in this valley for

many years, but this time of good living had ended when the last four winters had lasted for far too long and had become increasingly bitter. Long cold winters were survivable, but not when they were combined with the summers that had been short, wet and cold; it was too much to bear. Hunting had become increasingly difficult and the foraging had taken ever longer, too long, to fill the food-baskets. The very old and the children were starting to die. Although the bison continued to migrate across the nearby plains, the mammoth were now few in number and no young ones accompanied the herds. For the tribe to survive, they had to leave these northern lands now and head far to the south while they were still strong enough to travel, and before the winter snow began to fall and trap them here in a northern wasteland.

As much as he dreaded it, Rat had chosen to be left behind to face the winter alone. He was old, but it was his lame leg that had condemned him: he would never be able to keep up with the others during the long walk south. He was struggling to keep back his feelings of desolation, but he had sworn to himself that he would not show his sadness to those leaving; it would be wrong to burden them further with guilt. Even when young and in his prime he had never been a handsome figure: being small and dark, slight of build and with a thin face, graced with a nose shaped like an eagle's beak. Now that he was old, grey of beard and hair, his face deeply lined by the years and with cheeks sunken through loss of teeth, he looked every bit as old as he felt on this day. The first to reach him was Dalkan, the tribe's Chief, along with the elders and their families. The Chief held up his hand to halt the tribe, out of breath he was glad of the rest for he was even older than his shaman. As Dalkan walked over to him, Rat saw how thin his chief looked and with it the thought of how right it was for them to leave now before the tribe slowly starved to death. Dalkan sat by him on the rock and for a while they silently watched the tribe waiting on the slope. Then, breaking the silence, Dalkan said his farewell words.

'You were a good shaman Rat: you knew when the fish would enter the river and when the great beasts would pass over the plains. I know you could not save your first woman, Asa, but your medicines saved many lives over the years, including those of my children. For that we are all grateful.'

He sat in silence for moments more while they watched those on the lower slopes begin climbing once more to join those halted at the head of the line.

'You always knew where and when to send the women and children foraging for berries and roots and, until these last few years when the great beasts no longer came with their young, your blessings on the hunts were good and for that I thank you. Your sacrifice of the young man to ask the Earth Mother to warm the seasons did not work for us though did it, perhaps she has abandoned us to suffer these last years of misery?'

He smiled at Rat, then placed his large hands on Rat's thin shoulders and looked him in the eyes.

'You did well for a man who could not hunt. We had a good life together you and I looking after the tribe, I will miss your good counsel and am sad that we must leave you behind. Even older than you are, I still hope to see this tribe live once more under a warm sun.'

Dalkan released his hold on Rat, who then pulled apart his robe and tapped on his misshapen leg.

'We both know that I could never walk so far on this, whether your old bones will carry you all the way I cannot say, but I hope that your back is warmed under that southern sun when you pass. You are wrong though, the Earth Mother has not abandoned us, she is watching over us now. I only hope that she keeps one eye on me also, still here, as she follows your progress south. I will need all the help that she can offer me, so that I may live through the coming winter alone and with enemies in the next valley.'

These enemies, the Grovi, were different, an older race of humans. More powerfully built than the Salar, they had lived in the north for a long time before the Salar arrived to settle in the next valley. For many years the tribes had only tolerated one another, but the efforts of the then youthful friends, Rat and Brak, had ensured that eventually they became allies, trading goods and sharing hunts. Years later, when Brak was Chief of the Grovi, his son was taken captive by the Salar, breaking the bond between the tribes. He had then furiously forbidden all contact between the tribes and never again spoke with Rat. Dalkan looked at Rat with concern.

'Brak may take his revenge if he finds you in the camp alone, so you must keep yourself hidden from the Grovi when we are gone. I am sorry that we could not leave you more food, I fear that you may soon starve Rat; there is no more food to be found in this valley. I hope that you survive here for as long as you wish and not a day more. Sing chants for our safe journey when you return to your fire.'

Rat nodded, folding his arms against the cold.

'I will and I will pray for you every day until I feel that you are all safe, but you have a new shaman now, make good use of her, trust Suffi's judgement, I have trained her as well as I can.' He smiled at his chief, then leaned in to him and in a quiet voice cautiously offered some advice, 'It would not harm to put some of your strongest men at the back of the line, the stragglers will need guarding my Chief.'

If Dalkan resented being given tactical advice by his shaman he hid it with a small nod of agreement, slapping Rat on the shoulder he then rose to rejoin at the head of the line and resume the march to the south. Rat was pleased to see that Dalkan's pride did not prevent him from sending some men back to the rear as they moved off again.

Following behind the Chief and the elders was the man who had been the cause of the conflict between the tribes, Brak's son, Trovi. Physically and facially very different from the other men, he was taller and more powerfully built. Over time he had been grudgingly accepted and valued in the tribe because he was such a good hunter. Nevertheless, he was often sullen and resentful that he had been forced to give up all contact with his tribe, having been forbidden to even go and see his father and family to say farewell before this trek began. With him were his Salar-born woman and a young boy, a child that was already showing signs of his father's sturdy build. He nodded to Rat as he passed, acknowledging that, while he resented the restrictions that the Salar had placed upon him, he knew that he owed his life to Rat's interventions, twice saving him from certain execution.

As Rat's three sons from his first woman, Asa, came level with him, they stopped to stand around him with their women and the grandchildren to speak their farewell words, a little shamefaced to be abandoning him here where he was likely to die long before spring returned. He stood awkwardly and wished them all well, hugging them and his grandchildren for the last time, then he placed a hand on the shoulder of the youngest grandchild for support as he sat down on his rock once more. He beckoned for his eldest son to come closer, then passed on the leadership of the family to him.

'You are now the head of this family, keep a watchful eye on them all and see to it that my woman,' he stopped and corrected himself. 'Loli, who *was* my woman, well I ask that you make sure that she and the child survive the journey and make a good living in the new camp.'

The sons exchanged glances but the eldest promised that he would do so, and that if anything should happen to him his brothers would take on the task. Asa, had died giving birth to his third son and for the last few years he had been living with a much younger woman, Loli. This had not been a happy relationship: she had a sharp tongue and had made it plain from the outset that she was not pleased to be with an old crippled man. She had shown him some respect last night by not, as she often did, sneaking out of their bed to join one of the younger males of the tribe, a small sacrifice when after this day she would be free of him forever. As they had lain together, she had not welcomed anything other than for him to hold her, but he had been grateful for that and to lay with her body naked against his made him happy in the moment, knowing that this was the last time he would lie with a woman. In the half-light of the coming morning he had pulled back the furs to look down on her and smilingly commit her young body to memory for whatever time he had left. She was not thin like everyone else in the tribe but plump, perhaps she had been taking food from more than one man.

As she came up the valley, he noticed that she was trailing at the back and walking with one of the young men that he suspected she went to visit at night. Strapped to her back was the baby that was probably not his own. He was surprised to find that he felt no jealously but instead was pleased that she would be protected by this man on the dangerous journey ahead. When she was level to where he sat she held up a hand for the man to stop, then came over to Rat, knelt before him and looked up into his face.

'I am leaving you now old man.'

She had been calling him 'old man' since before they had come together, and while at first it was said with some small affection, over the years it had changed to a more contemptuous tone. Today, the words 'old man' had a tenderness in them. She knew that he had cared for her as well as he could, allowing her to leave him in the night without angry words the following day.

Although she was trying to hide it, she was thrilled to be starting her life afresh with a new man. For his part, Rat had never loved her as he had Asa but he knew that he would miss her, her smiles and her laughter, never laughing more than when she gossiped with the other women. He often suspected that the more raucous laughter was about him. He would miss the way that she wove summer flowers into her hair and her smell, the smell that she gave off now as she leaned in to kiss him on the cheek.

As her lips brushed against him he felt the softness of her face between her hair and where her furs rose around her neck. Looking into her wide brown eyes, he was very aware that these were the last human eyes he would ever look into so deeply, and was grateful that what he saw there was kindness.

'I have left you firewood and you'll find some meat in a cooking pot by the fire. Do not fall asleep and burn it as you usually do,' she chided him with a half smile.

She knew that he was likely to die during the coming winter, that he would know this, and felt more pity for him than she had expected to feel when the time came to say goodbye. She turned her shoulders sideways to present the baby to Rat.

'Here, kiss your baby goodbye and give your shaman's blessing on us both, that we will live and prosper on the journey and our new life.'

Leaning forwards to kiss the baby, he took its hand in his.

'I bless you both and I will say special prayers for you when I return to the camp. I know that you will both survive to reach the new lands in the south, and in the years to come you will have many babies to suckle. Finally, you will become a toothless and bad-tempered old grandmother before the Earth Mother comes to claim you back. Goodbye woman, take good care of the baby and have a happy life.'

She rose, kissed him on the forehead, then walked over to rejoin the man and the tribe. Rat shouted after her,

'Move up, move up, do not trail at the back, be at the middle of the line, it is the safest place to be, hurry yourself.'

Many of the tribe were breathless by the time that they reached him and, as most had said their farewells the night before, they only paused to nod to him as they passed. As he looked further down the valley he saw his protégé Suffi at the rear of the line. With two young boys by her side to slow her down and an enormous bundle on her back, she was moving steadily upwards with confident steps as she made her way to his side. He smiled with pride and affection for her; she would be the one to care for this tribe as their shaman throughout the many unforeseeable dangers that lay ahead for them. As she came up to him she cast aside her bundle, sat the infants down in front of him, then took her place beside him on the rock.

'Hello Uncle.'

'No Suffi, it is 'goodbye Uncle', this is when we part forever. From this time you are the Shaman of this tribe, you know that you are ready. I am sorry that no man has yet taken you to be his woman. Perhaps when you settle in the south a man may be found strong and wise enough to join with you and raise these boys.'

They turned to face each other and Rat was, as always, impressed by how striking she looked: tall and with the firm body of a hunter. She had high cheekbones and an attractive face, but she always grew her long black hair to hang over the left side of her face. He reached out and tucked that fall of hair behind her ear to expose the dull whiteness of her one blind eye. She put up a hand to cover the eye but he caught her wrist and stopped her.

'You are beautiful Suffi, do not hide behind your hair. You see more with that one good eye of yours than most do with two.'

He pulled her hand down to her lap, then took the other to hold. She was so grief-stricken to be leaving him that she struggled to smile as she wanted to.

'Well Uncle, as for having a man, I have the best of it do I not? I share my bed when I want and I sleep alone when I want, and nobody tells me what I should be doing, well, except for you.'

Rat nodded his understanding, releasing her hands he took from his robes a leather pouch which he opened to reveal the small squat figure of a woman that had been carved from stone, the Earth Mother.

'Here she is, as I promised you. Take her from me, she is yours now until you reach the end of your life. You will need her blessings on the tribe in the years ahead; guard her carefully. The tribe has held her for many years and you know that she is the most sacred object that we possess.'

She took the statue from him, examined it closely as she turned it over in her hands then placed it carefully back in its pouch and tied it around her neck.

'Do not worry, I will keep her safe all of my life and pass her on to the right one when the time comes.'

They smiled at one another, comfortable enough in their affection to speak only the truth. She placed a gentle hand on his arm.

'You are not likely to survive here Uncle, if the cold does not kill you, Brak may do if he finds out that you are alone. I will pray for you when I can and ask the Earth Mother to look after you.'

Looking up she realised that, apart from the rearguard, the tribe were gone and that she and her boys must leave at once to catch them up, so she threw an arm over his shoulder, pulled him to her and kissed his cheek. Then spoke briskly to her children.

'Say farewell to Uncle Rat boys, we must be gone.'

The boys stood and came over to Rat and hugged him, then Suffi slung the sack once more over her shoulders, taking a hand from each boy in her own she turned to resume the climb. Just before she disappeared over the ridge she looked back to see that he was staring at the ground in front of him, no doubt plucking up the courage to make his way alone down to the camp. She was about to turn back to the path when at last he looked up to where she was standing and waved an arm to her, she waved her final farewell to him then turned her back on him and vanished from sight. Now totally alone, he stood with difficulty, stumbling with the stiffness in his joints and his painful left leg. With two hands he tried to rub some feeling back into his cold backside. Far away below he could see the camp, now empty of life, and the only movement in all of the lower valley was a thin strand of smoke rising above the trees from the small fire that Loli had left for him.

2

RAT ALONE

It was late afternoon when Rat eventually limped back to the deserted camp and entered his round-house. Constructed from woven together wooden poles and covered by skins, with a floor that had been dug as deep as a man's knee, it had been just big enough for his family to live in but felt too large and empty now that he was alone. The smell from the pine twigs covering the floor made him think of Loli.

He damped down the fire: he had to conserve his stock of wood but he was also afraid that if the Grovi saw that there was still one fire in an otherwise empty camp they would become curious and enter the valley to see who remained. If they came they would find one man left behind, a man that their Chief hated. He was not at all sure whether Brak might seek to revenge the loss of his son and kill him. Even though he knew that he might not survive the winter, he did not want to leave his life by having his skull smashed in by

Brak's axe.

He decided to pray and chant before his feelings of desolation caused his courage to ebb away altogether. He chanted and prayed for his sons and his tribe, he chanted and prayed for Loli and her baby. Then, as he had done for many years, before and after they had parted as enemies, he chanted and prayed for Brak and his tribe. When he was done he carefully removed his shaman's robes and laid them in a reed box; without his robes he suddenly felt very mortal and weak. Taking some furs and his spear he went outside, placed the furs on the ground and lay on them for the remainder of the day, cloud-watching as he had as a child. As the short afternoon wore on he could feel the temperature dropping: the cool summer had turned now to an increasingly cold late autumn. He went back into the round-house, picked up a bowl of meaty bones and returned to his resting spot. Sitting up he pulled a fur around himself, chewed on the bones and thought about his life and his happy days and sorrows.

Being crippled from birth had distanced him from the other boys. He could never keep up with them when they ran around the camp playing hunting and war games. Inevitably they would taunt him for his weakness, so instead of keeping company with the men and boys he found himself staying with his mother and with the women of the tribe. They were kinder to him and taught him how to forage for roots, mushrooms and berries. It was under their instruction that he first began to understand what the medicinal properties of the various plants were. As he grew older and could understand what was being said, he was shocked at what the women would talk about, what they would do with the men in their beds, belittling those who failed to live up to expectations: either for their poor hunting prowess, or for a lack of stamina in the night.

He was not the only man who spent his days with the women. The tribe's Shaman, Sabal, when he wasn't mixing potions, was happy to spend his time gossiping and laughing with his female companions. The men of the tribe were content to go off and leave him with the women, confident that he was not interested in them, being more like a woman than a man. His mannerisms were an exaggeration of womanly gestures and his voice was high and somewhat shrill. He wept more easily than the women and had no violence in him at all. Rarely showing anger, even when dealing with badly behaved children. When he was still very young, Rat realised that only by befriending and learning from Sabal would he find his place in the tribe and prosper. He would become a shaman.

He made Sabal his friend and learned from him in the years that followed. At first he was shown the making of potions and medicines, and which plants, insects and animal parts could cure diseases. He would go with Sabal on his collecting trips, having to limp as fast as he could to keep up with him. They would spend days and nights together in the wild, and around the campfire at night Sabal would tell him stories from the history of the tribe and the ways of all the wild creatures around them. There was a lot to learn, but he knew that his future in the tribe was dependent on his learning all that Sabal would teach him, to become the best shaman that he could be.

When Rat was much older, Sabal introduced him to mushrooms, berries and plants that could take him on mysterious journeys. These were the deepest shamanic secrets, not to be shared with anyone not trained in such magic. Sometimes they would go up into the mountains, or deep into the forest and, while the other would watch and act as a protective guard, take it in turns to go on such journeys. Afterwards, they would discuss their strange dream journeys and the significance of what they had seen there. Usually Rat would have wonderful visions that left him feeling that he was in touch with the whole fabric of the world and that he could talk with the Earth Mother. But other dream journeys could be dark and full of fear and pain. He would come back shaken and desolate, understanding that there was no Earth Mother, only death and emptiness.

Sabal explained to him that these dream journeys, both the beautiful and the cruel ones, were showing him that this was what life really was behind day-to-day existence. He and Rat were stepping into an invisible world that surrounded the seen world, and controlled what men did without their being aware of what was all around them. It was the duty of shamans to take these journeys on behalf of the tribe, to experience the beauty and the pain and to translate their meanings for ordinary men and women.

Sabal said that they must be naked during these times and would often become erect and insisted on showing Rat how to take his member and pull on it until he ejaculated. He said that the fluid collected during such times had magical properties and would make special medicine. Rat was not sure that this was true and as he became older he increasingly suspected that Sabal, who did not lie with women, was using him. He also wondered what Sabal might be doing to him while he was having a dream journey, especially those dreams where he had sexual experiences. Then one night Rat decided that this must stop; when Sabal beckoned him to join him and play with his erect member Rat shook his head.

'No more Sabal, play with yourself if you must, but I will not be the one to make you come. I still want to spend my time with you, but as for that I would rather be with a proper woman, not with a man who thinks like one.'

Sabal only nodded, as if he had expected that it

would end eventually and it was never mentioned again. Rat chose to take his future dream journeys alone, or with his mother keeping guard for him.

Whenever he remembered the small boy that he had once been he became unsettled, for he had never forgotten that he was lucky to have been allowed to live when his parents saw that his leg was deformed. It was his mother who had refused to let Sabal leave him in the forest to die, and she had to convince both her man and Sabal to let him live. They had insisted that he could never make a life for himself, nor would he survive if expelled from the tribe as a teenager as so many boys were. He sighed at his memories and felt the loss of his kindly but strong mother, who had never spoiled him or protected him from bullying, but who had insisted that he do his very best physically despite his infirmity. She had also instilled in him an understanding of how to win people over with what he had to say: to charm where possible, but if that did not work, to use a sharp tongue to cut them down.

But here he was now, an old man, alone, and the only humans nearby were a hostile tribe in the next valley. He wondered what would be the cause of his death, starvation, animal attack, the approaching cold, or at the hands of the Grovi. As he sat, he pondered on which was the preferable death and whether he could defend himself from any of them. Starvation, or succumbing to the cold were his preferred choices, slow but relatively painless. At least death at the hands of Brak would be much quicker than any he could expect from the wolves. All too often, he had seen the pitifully slow deaths of creatures attacked by them: sometimes being slowly consumed from the rear while gazing at the sky in desperation, helpless to escape, only dying at last when their hearts were ripped from their bodies. He hardly dare contemplate being attacked by a wolverine, the worst possible of all the deaths that could come to him.

No, he would starve or freeze before he allowed himself to be taken by animals. He could only hope that the Grovi would not discover that he remained alone in the deserted camp. A small part of him hoped he would survive the coming winter, impossible as that might be, and perhaps live on in the year to follow. However, he did not know if he wanted to live at all without the companionship that came from being born and brought up in a tribe, where not one moment from birth to death was spent alone. So immersed was he in his tribe that it seemed that he could not separate his single self from that of the entire tribe. No one was indivisible from the whole in thought or deed. One of first shamanic lessons that Sabal had taught him was that the surest way to do harm to an enemy within the tribe was to isolate them from the others, either by whispered words, or by publicly denouncing them to the whole tribe. They would sicken in their isolation and become too mentally and physically weak to survive their loneliness; many would stop eating and die, or wander off into the wilderness.

His eyes had been closed while he had been remembering times past, but when he opened them, in the corner of his right eye he caught a movement. On the edge of the encampment, by the midden where the tribe threw their waste of bones, shells and skin, was the dark shape of the female wolf he had named Roden; she was the only wolf that ever came near the camp during daylight. She was tolerated by the tribe and seemed to recognise this. Sometimes, after scraping through the midden and eating some scrap or other, she would sit and watch the tribe going about their daily chores, until she became bored and left the camp to make her way back up to the high passes to rejoin her pack.

Rat had studied the wolves of the local pack since he was a boy and had given names to them all, their leaders and their followers. Over the years he had seen many wolves claim the top position, eventually to be killed or expelled from the pack by a usurper. The leader of the pack now, Groden, was the largest male that Rat had ever seen. He hunted with intelligence and had kept his pack alive during these lean years in the north. However, he and his pack had become bold with the lack of food and were increasingly fearless of men. Rat was sure that it was Groden's pack that had raided the tribe's burial site in the forest and eaten the flesh of the dead.

Roden was a different wolf, she did not seem aggressive and was observant of humans. She was an active member of her pack and hunted well, but when she came back from the hunt, particularly when the hunt had been unsuccessful, she would make her way down to the camp. This day she was again sitting and watching, but this time her gaze was fixed on Rat. He felt no threat from her, he only felt amusement that she seemed to be trying to work out why he was alone and where his pack must be. He shouted out to her.

'Hello there wolf, I am on my own, do you want to come and be my friend, we will make a new tribe together, just you and me, what do you say?'

She yawned and lay down, still watching him. He pulled a bone from the pot and waved it over his head.

'Do you want this little Roden, eh?'

Even as he did this, he thought, 'do not give it to the wolf, you may need to gnaw on it yourself before you are done here'. But he felt light headed with hunger and the loneliness, perhaps he could swap this bone for companionship of a sort. He was too far away to throw the bone to her, and was very aware that if he stood and walked towards her his hobbled walk might trigger her hunting instincts and she would attack him. So he lay down, hugged his spear along the length of his body and rolled towards the wolf, speaking to her as he rolled.

'It is alright little one, I mean you no harm. I have a gift for you.'

Roden sat up, now tense and leaning forward slightly, with a lowered head her gaze became very focused upon him.

Rat was frightened as he rolled, as during each roll his back was turned to the wolf, half expecting that he would complete a roll to find himself gazing up into those golden eyes. When he could not roll again for fear that this might happen, he stopped and sat up facing the wolf. Neither moved, then very slowly he raised his arm and threw the bone in an arc to land in front of Roden. She continued to stare at him for a long time then looked down to see what was before her. When he saw that, Rat rolled back up to the furs, finding it tougher going as he was now rolling uphill. When he arrived back at his starting point he sat up to find that she was gone, taking the bone with her. Exhausted now, he picked up the furs and the pot and limped back to the round-house, throwing the furs down where he and

Loli had lain together this morning. He tried to sleep but he slept fitfully, wakening often to tend the embers of his fire. With no other fires to take light from, he would do his best to sustain this one and so avoid the work of starting a fresh fire. It was a long and lonely night before the new dawn.

3

THE LEAVING OF BRAK

Alone in his camp on the second day after his tribe had left, Rat was not aware that the Grovi were about to depart their valley to head to southern lands. They were also leaving one man behind, his former friend, now enemy, Brak, who was too old to travel so far and with sight that was failing him. Although now looking old and thin from the last years of famine, and with his formerly red hair turned grey, Brak still carried himself like a chief. His bony frame was still broad, suggesting how powerful he had been as a young man.

His hunters had reported that the Salar had disappeared from their valley and left no one behind. Rat was being careful to keep his fire low and almost smoke free, so from a distance there was nothing to be seen, just an abandoned camp without any sign of life. Much as he had come to distrust the Salar and to feel hatred for Rat, a part of Brak also felt a loss that he would now never again see the man who had once been his friend. Their leaving was final confirmation for him that sending his own tribe south was now the only way to keep them alive.

With his aching limbs and short sight, Brak knew that he would never survive the long trek, or even make it back to camp from the high pass alone if he escorted them there for a final farewell. So when the time came, he had to say his farewells by his hearth in the long-house that was shared by all the tribe. He wished that his son Trovi could have replaced him as Chief, but Trovi had been forced to abandon his own tribe and live with Salars, something that caused Brak to hate the Salar and his childhood friend Rat in particular from that time. So it was that Brak selected Gaden, his adopted son, to replace himself as Chief and spent most of the remaining night counselling him on all of the knowledge that he would need to lead the Grovi in the years to come. How to balance the various factions and family power struggles in the tribe, how to delegate his authority without causing resentment and how to avoid bitter feuds from developing. It would be a difficult task on the long march south. He also warned him that he should not have any dealings with the Salar if their paths crossed, they were not to be trusted; then he gave him a final embrace and wished him well.

Just before the hard years had come to the valleys, Brak's son Trovi had disappeared for three days and despite many searches had not been found. On the fourth day a group of Salar hunters appeared on the ridge that separated the two valleys, then came part of the way down the slope, waving and pointing to indicate that they wanted to parley back up on the ridge-top. Taking their weapons with them, Brak, Gaden, and four hunters followed the party up to meet with the Salar. When they arrived at a rocky outcrop there, he was pleased to see that his friend Rat was sitting on a rock surrounded by his men. Rat waved the men away and beckoned Brak to come forward alone and to sit on a rock opposite from him. Rat smiled at Brak, then spoke to him in his own language.

'Greetings Brak, friend, it is good to see you again. Do you remember first meeting here when we were children?'

Rat had been eight summers old when one day he had become bored watching the other children shouting and running around, trying, but failing, to catch ground squirrels. He looked up at the heights of the valley ridge and wondered what he would see from up there, perhaps he could look down on the camp of the Grovi. He set off at his slow pace, hobbling on his weak left leg and gritting his teeth at the discomfort to keep heading upwards through the trees. When they saw what he was doing the other children called after him to come back, there could be wolves up there. Wolves often used the high passes, for the same reason as human hunters did, to look down into the valleys and search out prey. But he ignored their calls and persisted on up the steep slope. After a considerable time he came to a final rise and then he was on the ridge, to the side of him was a cluster of large rocks. The wind was strong and fresh up here, colder than in the valley and smelling of the sea.

He crossed the ridge and looked down on the valley where the Grovi had settled. In the distance, some way back from where the valley reached the sea, he could make out their camp. He was keeping a watchful eye out for wolves but, luckily, today he seemed to be alone on this windblown spot. He turned and walked back to the tumble of rocks; seeking a way through them he came to a finely grassed area, that was sheltered from the buffeting wind and was dotted with flowers of all colours. He saw that there was an opening in one of the rock walls and peered through it to see that there was a cave stretching away into the darkness, he was not tempted to go in there alone. Instead, he returned to the grass and the flowers, lay down on the colourful bed and looked up at the white clouds as they blew by so quickly in the brilliant blue sky. After a while it felt as if the clouds were stationary and he and the ground beneath him were hurtling along beneath the sky. He closed his eyes and rested.

When he opened his eyes he saw that an older boy was standing at his feet looking down on him. He was a little older than Rat, powerfully built and dressed in only a leather kilt. In his right hand he held, and was gently swinging, a stone-headed axe. Rat knew that he could not outrun this stranger, nor could he expect to beat him in a fight. Still on his back he scrambled away and then rose to his feet. Standing face to face now, neither moved, only the axe continued to move gently back and forth. Perhaps because he was so frightened for his life, Rat let out a loud fart that reverberated around the surrounding stone walls. The stranger continued to study him with an unblinking stare, then he smiled and started to quietly laugh. Nervously at first, Rat began to giggle. Brak slapped his chest.

'Brak.'

Rat pointed to his own chest.

'Rat.'

Then Brak dropped his axe, crouched, thrust his hands palm out and opened his eyes wide, then he rolled his eyes around in their sockets and waggled his tongue around while rocking his head from side. Rat was shocked at first, then found the effect so comical that he burst out laughing, Brak grinned back.

'Yes Rat, I remember meeting you here when we were children. I remember the many things we did together. But today I am seeking for my son, he has not returned home to us for three days, have you seen my boy Trovi?'

Rat sighed and frowned while tugging at his beard.

'I have and he is alive, although covered in bruises at the moment. He is our prisoner and will be bound to our tribe from now and ever after.'

The men from the Salar could not understand what Rat was saying to Brak, but knowing that Trovi was their prisoner they were expecting a violent response from the Grovi. The Grovi men understood very well what was being said, and while waiting for Brak's reply slowly made ready their spears and axes. Seeing this, the Salar men also lifted up their spears and hefted their weapons. Brak's barked response was so urgent and guttural that the Salar men had little doubt what was being said to their Shaman.

'You will have a good reason for this, or men will be dying today.'

Rat leaned forwards, knowing that what he said now would be critical to avoid a bloodbath.

'Listen to me Brak and think on our long friendship before you attack. We have good reason and Trovi is fortunate to still be alive today. He attacked and tried to mount one of our girls.' He gave a small smile. 'Perhaps he takes after his father too much.'

Brak just stared at Rat.

'He was only stopped when the other women heard her screams and set upon him. They considered killing him then, but instead tied him up and dragged him back to the camp to be dealt with by the tribal elders.'

He paused, scratched his beard and tugged at his hair. Then, having marshalled his thoughts continued.

'The tribal council sentenced him to be put to death yesterday, but in recognition of the way our two tribes have lived peacefully alongside each other for many years, and that we have shared hunting and trade, he was granted life. But Brak, he must be punished for this, and in return for his life we have taken his future, he has had to swear never to have contact with you or your tribe at peril of causing a war between our tribes.'

Brak nodded in understanding, then leaning forward in supplication and with lowered voice said,

'Give my boy back to me Rat and I will punish him; he is my only true son but I will deal with him severely, if only you will give him back to me.'

Rat would have done so, but the tribal council had made its ruling, this was the way it must be. He wanted to soften the blow by explaining to Brak that it was his intervention as Shaman that had saved the life of his son, but he knew that now was not the time.

'I cannot give him back to you, the decision has been made and I cannot go against the other tribal elders, even for a friend.'

He pleaded with Brak.

'Trovi will have a good life with us. Let him go and I will see that he does well in his new tribe. It is because you and I have been such close friends that the two tribes have never fought each other. I would wish it to stay this way Brak, say that you agree with me.'

Brak stood, broke the head from his spear and threw the shaft down between them. Clutching the spearhead in one hand he pointed it at Rat.

'There is to be no more friendship between Brak and Rat or the Grovi and the Salar. Our men will never hunt, or our women forage together with yours from this day onwards, your people must stay away from my valley or they will be attacked and killed on sight. You may continue to hunt on the plains but we will not run there with the Salar again. Do you understand?'

And so it was, Brak turned away, signalling for his men to follow he left the ridge and descended back into his own valley. Thereafter the tribes kept their distance from each other, and despite having been such close friends Rat and Brak never met again. They both felt the loss of the love they had once felt for each other.

Brak's woman, Culu, and two of his grandchildren had died in the last unrelenting winter. But on the morning of the march, he had his daughters and his remaining grandchildren to say a final goodbye to. They had gathered as much food as they could spare for him and a supply of firewood. Sat by his hearth, he hugged his daughters and their children and told them not to think of him as they journeyed south, he would do very well here on his own. Beaming at his grandchildren he picked up a bowl containing mushrooms and berries.

'I am thinking that perhaps you chicks picked these delicious morsels for your grandfather. They look perfect for me to eat by the fire tonight when you are all gone. I will think of you all out there on the plains while I am eating this food, safe, cosy and warm by my hearth. You must all be brave and do everything that your mothers and your new Chief ask of you.'

He looked around at each of his grandchildren.

'Will you do that for your grandfather, eh, will you be brave and follow orders?'

The grandchildren solemnly nodded. Turning to look at his daughters, he sought to reassure them also.

'Do not grieve for me girls, I have lived a wonderful life, most of it with a great woman, your mother. What more could I have asked for that was not given to me? If I die I will go happily, and if I live I will be no longer be a chief of men but the chief of all the animals, birds and flowers in the valley instead,' then while smiling around at them all he thought, 'may they listen to my words more than my tribe ever did.'

His daughters had placed a seat outside of the doorway of the long-house, so that he could watch with blurred sight as his tribe left the camp. One of his granddaughters ran back to him to give him a final hug, before he pulled her arms away from his neck and sent her to her mother with a gentle slap on her backside. Although they soon disappeared from his sight, he sat there waving an arm just in case one of them should look back. The Salar had left before his own tribe, so now he knew for certain that he was going to be the last man left alive in the north. He felt overcome with desolation and loneliness and the thought of his own, soon to come, death.

4

BRAK ALONE

As with every member of the two tribes, Brak had never been without constant companionship. From birth to death and throughout a life, the tribe was indivisible from any individual, life sustaining life. For the first time since the long-house had been built there was now only silence, no voices raised in argument, no women laughing, no children shouting in play or babies crying for attention. For generations the whole tribe had lived in this one room, built long ago from mammoth bones and wood and roofed with turf. It had always been smoky and noisy and still contained all the smells of the tribe's life in the valley.

He found it overwhelming, he could not stay in there. To escape his memories he took some burning sticks from the fire to set another fire to burn outside, then he collected some furs and went outside to take a seat by the fire. The only sound was that of the chill wind coming in from the sea, making the tree-tops sigh as it passed through the valley. As night fell the wind brought a sea-fret, rolling banks of mist that covered the trees in shrouds of droplets. A scene that Brak could not see, only feeling the moisture condense on his face, beard and hair, isolating him further in the tiny island of light around his dying fire, surrounded on all sides by the vast darkness.

He decided to die this night. He removed all of his clothing and lay naked on his back on the bare earth. Running his hands down his body he could feel all of his ribs through his thin skin, and clasping his arms he felt the loss of the muscles that had made him such a fierce warrior and hunter in his youth. His legs were no longer powerful but thin like those of a young girl. There had been a time when he had been proud of his fat stomach, proof of his prowess as a hunter, but now his stomach dipped almost to his backbone. He was not afraid to die. Unlike the Salar, the Grovi had no religion, no belief in an Earth Mother or any other god. Instead, their spirituality lay in being in tune with their place in the living world and seeking always to resonate their lives with the land and the creatures around them, showing respect to fallen animals and beaten enemies alike. Though death was always present, it was seen as the final step in a life and nothing more. However, they still felt the grief of loss, especially with children and loved ones who were cherished: there was always pain at their going, never to be held or seen again. But all must die, and the old in particular were often relieved to finally leave behind the pains of life.

He lay there trying to die, breathing out all of the air in his lungs then holding his breath until he almost passed out, but each time he would relent, gasping when the cold damp air came rushing back into his body. Then he thought of cutting his throat with his flint knife, the way he would ease the life from a wounded deer. He sat up and took from his belt the knife given to him by Rat when they were young men. He felt its razor edge and taking it in one hand lay back down again. With one hand pulling his beard out of the way, he pushed the blade against his neck on the opposite side to his knife arm and pressed down, then drew it across his neck. There was much more pain than he had expected and the shock of it made him stop. He could feel blood run between his fingers and down the side of his neck, the smell of the blood bringing with it memories of successful hunts. He could not do it, perhaps he was not as ready for death as he had thought. A tiny part of him would not give up on living and breathing but what had he to live for? He had no tribe, he had no family, he was no longer a chief; he was just a lonely human shell now and that shell was failing him. He could not even see clearly, he would surely die soon anyway, but still he wanted to live to see another day. He reached out for his furs and covered himself.

He lay there motionless until the morning came and with it some warmth from the sun. He lay there all morning as the cold left the deepest parts of his body, and he had to close his eyes and turn his face away to shield them from the bright disc of the sun. He had not wept since his Culu had passed, so he was surprised to find a tear starting from the corner of his left eye, then more rose in the right and then both eyes, until they trickled down the sides of his face, mingling with the blood on his neck. 'What is this', he thought, 'am I turning into a child who cries for his mother?'

He fell asleep and dreamt. He was a baby, being

carried on his mother's back while she foraged for food with the other women. When she stooped to pick berries he found himself tilted forwards, watching her busy hands as she chatted constantly with her unseen companions, then when she stood he was tilted back, squinting against the sun, back and forwards, back and forwards, till he fell asleep and found himself to be now a young boy playing with Rat in the sea, which Rat feared but was a second home to Brak. They ran from the sea and up the beach and in the running he found himself on the hunting-plains running after vast herds of bison, clutching a spear and whooping with the sheer thrill of living. Then he was a young man, full of power and mastery of his world, with a beautiful young wife, Culu, waiting for him with their children as he returned laden heavily with meat from a hunt. If there had been anyone there to see him, they would have seen that he was smiling in his sleep as the tears dried. When he woke the dreaming time had done its work, and the golden memories of his youth stayed with him in the first few moments of regaining a full awareness of where he was.

He was hungry. Hunger had been a constant for the whole of the lean times, but he knew that this was a hunger that could not be ignored, it would kill him. He had to go back to the long-house and see what his daughters had left for him. In a bowl lined with moss he found dried fish, whose strong smell caused him to wrinkle his nose. In another bowl were pieces of meat, half a heart and the liver of a deer; in the final bowl were the mushrooms and berries picked by his granddaughters as their final gift to their grandfather. He chose the fish to eat for his meal this day. Still feeling too uncomfortable to remain in the long-house, he returned to his seat outside, where he cradled the bowl in his lap and sucked the flesh from the fish bones. Although the smell was bad, the taste was good and he could soon feel his body welcoming the food and dampening the hunger for the present.

He chewed on the skin, which was not easy as he lacked many of his teeth. Then he turned the head of the fish over in his fingers looking for something edible, but the effect of the drying had destroyed the eyes and the brain, so, against his own strict rule that all waste must be taken to the midden, he tossed the head over his shoulder to be caught in one silent bite by the wolf Roden who was sitting behind him. She had been watching him since before he woke, and her sense that he was in some way weak and unseeing made her feel comfortable enough to sit close by him. Unknowing of his companion, Brak picked up a twig and took his time scraping the fish-scales from his teeth, then he took a sip of water and lay back down, allowing the food to take its effect while trying to warm his body through. Roden also lay down, so relaxed was she that she rolled onto her side and stretched out to her full length, a length that was longer than Brak was tall, before yawning and quietly watching Brak through half closed eyes.

Brak drifted in and out of a dozing half-awake sleep. There was comfort here, he was not old, cold, hungry or dying. Consciously, he drew upon his greatest memory of the past to bring him strength in his present. He had been a young man, already recognised within the tribe as one of two or three young men who might one day become a future tribal leader. He had proven himself in many ways as a hunter, brave and fast in the hunt, but so were his rivals. He required a deed that would set him as one apart. Then one day in spring, as part of a small hunting party, he had been hunting along the edge of the sea. The collecting of shellfish and crabs fed the tribe well but was regarded as the work of young boys and girls. Today, they were looking for seals, a difficult prey that would bolt for the water where they were impossible to catch. But Brak and his friends knew where the seals bred on a large rock-shelf under a high cliff, a cliff that would have to be climbed down to reach the young pups, who were then easy to catch and kill.

They knew the safest route, still dangerous, but being young and fit they all managed to reach the base of the cliff together. They stopped there a while and ate the birds eggs they had collected on the way down. The seals made a terrible noise at their approach, the mothers torn between fleeing for the sea or staying to defend their pups. The bull seal had no such hesitation; he chased the hunters across the rock-shelf, braying and snapping at them while they laughingly danced out of his way. It took only a short time to kill as many pups as they could safely carry back up the cliff, one for each hunter.

They stored the bodies at the base of the cliff then, at Brak's cajoling, walked around the seal colony to where a rocky ledge jutted out into the deep sea. Brak was not sure why he had brought them here, but it felt good to be so far out from the grassy land and on the border between rock and the unknown depths.

The sea was glassy smooth, with a gently rolling swell where sunlight sparkled across its surface; it felt good to be here. Then they heard it, a burst of discharged air from out of sight around the corner, then another and another. They knew what was coming, every spring the great creatures could be seen swimming where the deep water met the rocky shore. Untouchable monsters of the deep, with enormous twisted spears protruding from their heads that were longer than a man was tall. Today they were passing so close to Brak's small group they could smell the breath of the creatures. In times past many had thrown spears at them but they rarely penetrated, and those that did would fall away as the creatures dived.

Without thinking, Brak left his party and ran to a place where the rocks rose high above the sea.

While climbing up as fast as he could, he could see the creatures starting to move directly beneath him. He reached the top, then leapt out, aiming for the shiny back and to land astride the beast. The fall knocked the wind out of him, but he knew that he must strike as he landed and brought his spear down two handed and with all of his force. The point of the spear drove in deeply and stuck there. The creature dove for the depths and Brak hung on as it went down. Opening his eyes he could see the creature's mottled back beneath him and the blood pouring away from where the spear had entered the flesh. His hair was whipped back by the force of the water, and as they went deeper he could feel the pain of the pressure in his ears; it took all of his strength to maintain a hold on the bending shaft of the spear. He lost his grip with his knees and his legs now trailed behind him, banging painfully on the back of the creature as it bucked to dislodge him.

He had swam and played in the sea since he was very young, developing an ability to hold his breath much longer than most in his tribe, but even so he knew that he was running out of air and would soon have to release his spear to make his way up to the surface. Just as he felt he was about to lose consciousness, the creature broached and he could fill his lungs with air. Pulling back on the spear he regained his grip with his knees, then pulled the spear out and drove it down once more, deeper this time. Then he lost his grip and the beast was gone, leaving him behind on the surface while it escaped once more into the deep with the spear still embedded in its head. He felt very tired and could barely swim his way back to the shore, where he was met and half-carried by his friends to be laid down on the rocks. When he had recovered they made their way back to the bottom of the cliff, loaded the seal pups onto their backs and made their way back to camp. The story of Brak's remarkable adventure was quickly shared with the tribe, but the old hunters gave the story little credit, assuming that the young men were simply bragging and exaggerating Brak's deed.

Two days later, the body of the narwhal washed up on the beach with Brak's spear still firmly embedded in its head. The whole tribe worked together to cut up the body and the strongly smelling meat fed them for weeks. No other hunter had ever achieved such a thing, and thereafter Brak's position within the tribe was unmatched. In the years to come many young hunters would try to emulate Brak, but none succeeded and one was killed by being dashed against the rocks. Brak thought it prudent to never try it again; he was content with his glory, and the stories about him and his deed had many a campfire storytelling. The tusk was cut away, cleaned of meat and mounted in the centre of the camp as a permanent reminder of the day that Brak had ridden the sea monster.

While Brak was remembering his shining moment, Roden had picked up on the scent of fish coming from him. She stood now, with her head lowered she gazed at his prone body, then slowly and with care she stepped towards him, her body now lowered to the same height as her head. She was soon at his side where the smell of fish was overwhelming, and now she could also smell the dried blood on his neck. She stood fully upright, peered down into his unmoving face and began sniffing gingerly at his mouth. Brak heard the noise and opened his eyes to find Roden's face blocking out the sky, her nose almost touching his mouth, her golden eyes staring into his. He screamed in terror, turning away his face and thrusting up his arms to push her head away but feeling only air. With eyes shut and his body in a tight ball, he windmilled his arms around his body and his head, all the while crying out and whimpering in fear. After a moment, and suffering no attack, he looked around but the wolf was gone.

It was not just his hands that shook, his whole body trembled with the shock of what had just happened to him. No wolf had been so bold before and the implication that he was not safe alone in the camp was frightening. His previous longing for death was replaced by a strong will to live, or at least a wish not to die in the jaws of a wolf. He returned once more to the long-house and with his hands still shaking reached for his fire-making stones, striking them again and again into tinder and dry moss. Capturing a spark, he cupped the moss and tinder in his hands and blew gently until they caught and he could relight his fire. Once lit, he sat awhile bent close over its protective shield until the heat drove him back. He went to the door and scanned all around; he knew it was pointless, with his blurred sight a whole pack of wolves could be sat watching him, just a stone's throw away, but he would not be able to see them. He gave up peering around and went back to the fire. Then he found his axe and spear and placed them next to his side; he must not make the mistake of allowing them to be out of his reach again. As he calmed down his breath became steady again. He smiled at his foolish pride, one moment daydream remembering his monster-killing prowess as a great warrior, then, in an instant, in the real here and now, a terrified and whimpering old man.

5

POLUS

When Rat awoke, for a moment he forgot that he was alone. He looked around the round-house listening for voices, seeking reassurance that the tribe leaving him behind had only been a dream. But there was no sound, no voices to be heard; this was no dream. He shivered with the cold, so feeding the dying fire with dry sticks to avoid making smoke he heated up stones, then holding them between two sticks dropped them into a leather bowl filled with water. When the water was hot, he poured some out into a small bowl to make a herbal drink that he knew would fortify and cheer him. As he drank he thought about what he would do in the coming days, how he could live alone through the winter. Did the Earth Mother still protect him, or was she now only watching over the Salar as they travelled south, leaving him abandoned? He wondered if she had forsaken him three years ago, after the ceremony he had given for her, nothing had gone well for the tribe since then.

Rat had learned well from Sabal, including memorising all of the ceremonies that must take place during the passing seasons. With Sabal at his side he had led many of these ceremonies and was comfortable in his new role in the tribe. However, there were ceremonies that were reserved for special times; ones that Sabal had explained to him but they had never performed together. The first time that he sacrificed someone was shortly after Sabal had died, when it was thought fitting to mark Rat being made the tribe's Shaman by sacrificing a young man. Killing the terrified boy had left its mark on Rat and he promised himself that, should he be called upon to do so again, the victim would go to the Earth Mother heavily drugged.

After the first lean year for the tribe, the Chief came to him to ask that he perform a ceremony to please the Earth Mother and break the time of impending famine. Rat would have to sacrifice another young man. To his dismay, he heard that the Chief had decided that Trovi would be the ideal man to play the central role in the ceremony. Occasionally, a single young man, or a small group of men, expelled by their own tribes at puberty, might find a tribe and seek permission to join them. It was then that the tribe would decide whether they would be allowed into the tribe, or whether they would be sent on their way, either to starve to death or to find sanctuary with another tribe. If rejected, these often starving young men were given a small amount of food and then escorted from the valley and warned never to return. More rarely, small bands of young men would sneak into a valley and try to carry away the younger women. Trying to escape while holding onto snarling, spitting young women invariably resulted in some, or all of them, being caught and killed.

Shortly after the Chief had asked Rat to perform the special ceremony, a young man of their own race was found sitting at some distance from the camp. He was sat by a trail, with his weapons laid on the ground in a gesture of peace to the tribe members who passed him as they went out hunting or foraging. He smiled at them but did not speak, he was obviously very nervous. Rat went out and stood before him. He seemed a well made young man with a friendly and open face, he smiled up at Rat. Rat smiled back a welcoming smile, this young man must have been sent here by the Earth Mother, he was exactly what Rat was looking for. The man was reassured to see that Rat was a small man and that he limped, it made him seem less threatening.

'Welcome young man, who are you, where have you come from and what do you want with us?'

When he answered, his speech was slightly different from that used by the Salar but perfectly understandable. He stammered in his nervousness.

'I, I, I am Polus, from a tribe far to the south and west of here, th, th, there was no place in the tribe for me and I have been sent out to make a life for myself and to see if any tribe may have a place for me. I am a good hunter and can even f, f, forage with the women if that is what you would want. I would be happy to join your tribe, doing whatever you would ask of me.'

'There is nothing to be frightened of Polus, I think that we can find a place for you in this tribe. We are the Salar and as their Shaman I welcome you to come into the camp. Come, I will take you to our Chief and see what he says. Give me your axe and spear until we have spoken with him.'

Polus stood, obviously much relieved, and handed his weapons to Rat. They walked into the camp, Polus walking slowly to match Rat's hobbling steps. When they came to the Chief's round-house Rat dropped Polus' weapons onto the ground. Then taking Polus by his elbow brought him before the Chief, who was seated and surrounded by some hunters and his sons. Rat pushed his way through them to stand in front of Dalkan.

'Make way, make way, I have an important visitor for our Chief, a young man who has come a long way to contribute to the future of the tribe.'

He turned and whispered to Polus.

'This is our Chief, Dalkan, he will say whether you can stay with us or not, so show him respect, as you would have done to your old Chief.'

Unseen by Polus, he winked at Dalkan before speaking.

'My Chief, you may remember that we spoke about our need for someone to ensure the future wellbeing of the tribe, well we have here someone who could be that man, do you think? It is as if he was sent here for that purpose.'

Dalkan, nodded to Polus then turned to Rat.

'Still trying to save Trovi's skin are you Rat?'

Not understanding, Polus looked at his companion who smiled reassurance to him, then Rat turned back to Dalkan.

'I made a promise to Brak that I would protect his son if he would give him up. I would choose to keep my word if you will agree.'

Polus felt uneasy at what was being said, who was this Trovi and what part was he to play in protecting a man he did not know? He spoke up and repeated to the Chief what he had said to Rat, that he was a fine hunter and would do whatever was asked of him. Dalkan found this amusing.

'So, you would do anything for this new tribe of yours would you boy?'

Enthusiastically, Polus spoke up.

'Oh yes, yes, I would commit my life to this tribe. All I have I will give and share, if only you will accept me and give me shelter.'

He heard some of the men sniggering at his words.

'Well,' said Dalkan. 'We cannot argue with that can we Rat? Is this what you want Shaman, you wish for this and you will take this man's, what shall we say, oath to serve, as a sign that he is suitable for our needs? If you really want him you may have him, but be sure that this is done well for all our sakes.'

'Thank you my Chief,'

He turned to Polus.

'Thank Dalkan for giving you this honour.'

Again Polus wondered at the words being used by these two men and the amusement he had seen on the faces of the hunters around them. But he expressed his thanks and smiled back at the men as Rat pulled him away and out of the round-house.

In the following days Polus was given the best of everything. Fine clothing and as much food as he could eat. Rat took him to meet all in the camp and everyone he met was friendly and welcoming. Only one little girl, a granddaughter of the Chief, was less than friendly. She refused to come to him when Rat tried to introduce her, instead she stood some distance away pointing to Polus. In a small sure voice she said,

'You are the man who is going to die.'

Polus was shocked that she would say such a thing but Rat laughed at her words.

'She is playing with you, she likes to speak warnings to strangers, pretending she is a chief like her grandfather, take no notice. She is just a child, come, there are others to meet.'

While meeting the members of the tribe, Rat introduced him to Bell, an attractive older woman whose man had been killed some years ago while hunting mammoth. She was so friendly that Polus quite forgot what the little girl had predicted for him. When the time came for Rat to take him away she stepped forward and whispered in his ear.

'Do not spend your night with Rat, come back here to me tonight and we can make each other happy, yes?'

He nodded that he would, not knowing that Rat had

already arranged this for him: to keep him as content and as happy as possible, and also to keep him far away from his own woman, Loli. While they were walking, Polus stopped Rat and looking him in the eyes said,

'I cannot thank you and the Salar enough for making me so welcome here. You have been kinder to me than my own tribe. They cast me out into the wilderness but you have taken me in. I can never repay your kindness.'

'We are pleased to have you Polus, tomorrow night we will be holding a feast in your honour and to make you a full tribal member.'

That night they had a very full meal prepared by Loli, after which Rat had pulled him close and whispered to him.

'My guess is that Bell asked that you join her tonight, off you go, enjoy this night for tomorrow night will be a greater one for you.'

And so it was that Polus stayed the night with Bell and spent the next day in the friendly company of Rat, the Chief and his hunters. He was a happy young man. When evening came, the tribe gathered around a great fire built in the centre of the camp. Two whole deer and a boar were roasted and shellfish were laid on wooden boards all around the fire. Before the feast began, the Chief asked Rat to come with Polus to stand before the fire, then asked Polus to swear his allegiance to the Salar and to the Earth Mother. Which he did, and then the Chief declared that Polus was now a full member of the tribe. Rat stepped forward and placed a thick braided leather necklace about his neck. Polus looked about, expecting to see similar necklaces in the watching crowd, but he seemed to be the only one so honoured. When the oaths were complete, Rat took Polus to one side and gestured for him to sit down while the women of the tribe brought him platters piled high with food. Rat sat on his right-hand side and a woman, with long black hair and wearing a black robe, sat to his left. Rat introduced him to her.

'This my friend is Suffi, she is my assistant.'

Suffi turned to look at him; although her hair obscured most of her face, he could see that she was strikingly beautiful. Rat handed him a deep bowl, filled with a liquid that shone amber in the firelight.

'Here, drink this my friend, you will feel wonderful.'

And so he did. The drink was bitter but after a short while he did feel wonderful, he had never felt so happy, so accepted. Rat left him for a while chatting happily with Suffi. When Rat returned, he was dressed in his shaman's robe, with his face painted and holding his mask in one hand. Rat was nervous, what he did tonight would be the focus of the whole tribe and for a while his status would be higher even than that of the Chief. To ensure that all went well, he had gone from family to family explaining to every member of the tribe their role in the time to come. He drank from his own bowl, a drink that was different from the one that he was giving to Polus. His own drink would help him to bridge the gap from this life to the Earth Mother and her world. On behalf of the tribe, he had to make that leap and speak to her across the divide.

He gave Polus some more drink and watched him carefully; it was important that he was at ease. Polus looked about at all the faces in the flickering light of the fire and was content, if a little dizzy from the effects of the drinks. As the night wore on he felt strange but happy, he looked about again and was surprised to see that all of the tribe were now watching him. He knew that this should feel wrong but for some reason it did not. He felt as though he was losing his grasp of time, as if it would sometimes stop, then suddenly lurch forward. He blinked and looked straight ahead to where he saw that the Chief's little granddaughter was now standing. She strode towards where he was sitting until she stood directly in front of him, stepping forward she pulled her hand back then slapped him across the face. He saw her do it but did not feel the blow, then he felt the pressure of the drinking bowl that Rat was holding to his lips and drank deeply from it.

He was now surrounded by the whole tribe and all were smiling at him. As he was pulled to his feet by Rat he saw that Rat was also smiling at him. He grinned back, then he felt a blow to his back which sent him staggering forward towards a powerfully built young man in front of him, who he knew to be Trovi. This man slapped him and then pushed him back into the crowd. He could not believe what was happening to him. He was hit from the side, then he was struck again from behind and once more went staggering towards the waiting Trovi. He realised that this must be some part of the initiation ceremony, to be performed before he became a full tribal member, so he continued smiling back at his attackers. Although he felt the blows, he felt no pain, it was as if it was all happening to someone else and not to him. The tribe were taking it in turns to strike him, not savage punches, but slaps to the head and elbows to his body. Then the blows became continuous, until he fell to his knees under the onslaught.

Suddenly it stopped, it was such a relief that it was over. Suffi stepped behind him and placed her hands on his shoulders to steady him. Polus tilted his head back and smiled up at her to see that she was staring down into his eyes, and he could see now that her left eye was entirely white. Her strange appearance made him want to giggle, but then he saw her step aside to be replaced by a masked figure. Looking up at that inhuman mask made him fearful, so he tilted his head forwards, looked at the ground and tried to steady his breathing. Then he looked up and saw that the little girl was standing in front of him again, on her outstretched palm was sitting the small carved figure of a woman. As Polus wondered if the girl was offering him the figure, Rat slipped a short stick down through the leather necklace around his neck and started twisting it. Polus' hands came up as he tried to pull the braided leather band away from his neck, but even as his fingers struggled to get a grip he lost consciousness and his head fell forwards.

Standing at his side, Suffi placed her hands around his chest to support his sagging body while Rat continued to turn the stick. The effect of the potion that Rat had drank now reached its peak and he felt as if he had left his body and was now standing where the girl was holding out the Earth Mother, watching himself strangling Polus. He watched as he stopped turning the stick, then releasing the pressure just before Polus' life left his body; pulling a flint knife from his belt he sliced across the young man's neck, using his other hand to hold the head back while pushing the body forward, so that his blood fell into a bowl held by Suffi.

A collective sigh went around the tribe but Rat did not hear it. He was with Polus, the two of them in one body and moving into the world of the Earth Mother. They stepped through a shimmering veil into the next life where Polus separated from him, stepping away before turning, whole once again, to raise his hand in a farewell gesture. Rat held up his hand in response and looked about for the Earth Mother, but she was nowhere to be seen, this was a desolate place. This had all been for her, he became frantic and ran around the stricken landscape looking for her. Looking back at Polus he saw a look of anguish on his face, he seemed lost.

Suddenly he found himself back in the real world, standing over the body of the young man. Suffi laid Polus gently down next to the bowl of blood which Rat picked up and offered between outstretched hands to the tribe, who each in turn dipped fingers into the blood to daub it on their faces and the faces of the children and babies. Two hunters stepped forward and bound Polus' hands and feet then slipped a branch through them, the way they would with the carcase of a deer, and carried him out of the camp. Two more hunters, carrying torches, led the way in the darkness as they walked in procession to the marshlands. Once there, they lowered one end of the branch into a deep pool and allowed the body of Polus to slip off into the depths.

6

SNOW

One week after the tribes had left their valleys, far out over the grey sea, clouds larger than mountains were sweeping down from the north. Their undersides were black but their tops shone white in the late afternoon sun. At first drifting separately, they slowly collided and coalesced until they blocked out the sun almost entirely. Just one shaft of light was left to shine brilliantly down through the increasing darkness and cause the surface of the sea to shimmer where it struck. Then the clouds closed this one window and shut out all the light, everything below them became sunless and in darkness. The cloud mass drifting towards the land now released snow which fell in large flakes, and as they fell towards the sea they were caught by a gentle wind that carried them inland, into the valleys that had once been home to the Salar and Grovi.

Rat was sat in a clearing in the camp, looking down the valley to the sea when he saw the snow flurries coming towards him. The flakes arrived gently, sticking to his face and his body, he sighed and thought, 'this is death coming for me, so quietly, so soon, sooner than I expected'. He looked around and saw that the ground and the side of the trees facing down the valley were turning white. He wondered if the snow would catch his tribe on the plains and how they would cope if it became too deep for the children to pass through. As he started turning white he said a prayer to the Earth Mother to spare them and allow them to travel on.

In his valley, Brak was standing outside of his long-house; he did not see the clouds, did not see the snow coming, but he knew the hush that came with snow and as he sensed it so he felt the first flakes landing on his eyelashes, then on his face. He rubbed his face with his hands and looked at the moisture that lay there. He could see the snow falling for a short distance all around and, like Rat, knew that this could be a disaster for his tribe. He went into the long-house and paced about, sometimes stopping to stroke the white mammoth bones that were part of the walls. Most had been built into the walls many years before his birth, but there were many that held memories for him, each one telling a different story of summers hunting on the plains. When he was a boy the Grovi had hunted alone, but his bond with Rat brought about the Grovi and Salar hunting together, until the tribes had fallen out. They had been good days and good nights. Even hauling the meat and the bones back to the main camp at the end of the hunting season was a happy time.

Ever since the Grovi had lived in their valley, they had moved in the summer to the hunting-plains to hunt bison and mammoth. Only the very old members of the tribe were left behind. One year, they returned to the main camp to find that all of the old ones had been killed and the few possessions that they had were taken. No one would ever know who had done this, and calls for guards to be left behind in future years failed, as who would stay behind to spend summer with the old ones and miss out on the wonderful hunting season? Everyone became excited when it was time to go. There was so much to do, weapons to be prepared, food baskets to fill, clothes to make and mend. The young men and women especially wanted to look their best when staying in the summer camp, for this was when most couples came together. The young men would try to outshine one another during the hunting, and especially in the loud boasting that followed when sat around camp-fires.

It was the only time that the tribe did not all sleep together in one long-house, but separated now into loose family groups that slept in yurts. The grandest one was the Chief's; enormous mammoth tusks, that had been collected over generations, were planted into the ground to create a hide-covered framework over a sunken floor that had been dug out of the plains. It was an ideal time for the young men to go visiting other yurts, where there might be an attractive one to gaze at over the firelight while talking with their family. This was how Brak came to be with Culu. He had known her since she was born, as children they had played together and she had always been friendly with him. However, on one summer camp when he had become a young man, he noticed that she seemed different, more grown up, even more attractive. He took to visiting her family with meat to share, which enabled him to brag how he had hunted that day and the bravery that it had taken. One night when sitting around their fire, holding forth to her father about how he had singlehandedly killed two bison that day, he noticed that Culu was giggling with her younger sister. He felt uneasy, he wished that Rat was here to give him advice but Rat did not travel to the hunting camps. He then launched into a detailed description of how he had killed the sea monster, looking about he was pleased to see that all seemed to be giving him close attention, even though they had heard this tale many times before. All except the two girls, who had now collapsed onto the ground, hugging each other and crying with laughter. Even stern words from their father could not stop them but seemed to make them worse.

Brak stopped talking and all waited in the awkward silence for the girls to pull themselves together. Brak sighed, her father coughed, the women smiled, other men coughed, as the girls continued trying to smother their laughter. Eventually, the girls calmed down and sat again by the fire, trying to look solemn but with faces that were still wet from the tears of laughter. Brak felt awkward, the conversation slowly dried up. Silence followed, then gathering his courage he spoke to her father.

'If your daughter, Culu, is willing, I would ask if she be allowed to come and live with me and my family in our yurt for the remainder of the summer-hunt. Then, if she wishes to stay with me after that we will take a hearth together in the long-house when we return to camp.'

They both looked to Culu, who smilingly nodded her willingness.

'Well Brak,' said her father, 'if you make her laugh, she will stay with you.' He looked at his wife and then at Culu, then smiled. 'But if you make her cry, then she will return to her family.'

Brak nodded.

'I will not make her cry, though I am not sure why I make her laugh so. Perhaps she will tell me when she is ready.'

And so it was that from that night on they were together, and Brak did not make her cry and she told him why he had made her laugh. He had talked so grandly about himself that night, that he had quite forgotten that her family were also skilled hunters: that very day her father had killed four bison. She had thought him foolish and funny, but he was a young man and young men were often foolish. She had seen something in him, she knew that one day he would be as special as he thought himself to be. Many years later, when she would hear Brak boasting to others of his hunting prowess, and yet once more of the day that he had killed the sea monster, she would smile to herself and think that while he would sometimes forget to be modest, he had finally become the great man and chief she had known he would be when they were young.

The mammoth bone that Brak had his hands on now was the one that he had carried back when that summer-hunt had ended, and he and Culu were given their own space in the long-house. Mammoths had walked across the plains for thousands of years before his tribe had hunted there, and the many that had died in all that time had left their bones to bleach white over the years. It was the custom for each man to carry back some of these bones to strengthen the walls of the long-house. The meat and hides had to be borne on the backs of the whole tribe, including those children that could walk alone. The yurts were buried in the ground, to be dug up again the following year. As much as he had loved her, Culu was now only a memory, though part of her was often seen in the gestures of his daughters and granddaughters, and in the red coral-bead necklace that he had kept of hers. The necklace had been a present he had given to her when they had been allowed their own hearth to sit by in the long-house. The days alone now found him starving. He had no more food and no wood for the fire. He felt very vulnerable going into the forest to pick up fallen wood when he could not see any danger. He had started to use his axe to break down the wooden sections of the walls of the long-house for firewood, destroying his only protection against the weather and the wolves.

In the adjacent valley, sitting in his round-house, Rat had come to a decision. He had no more food and the little that he could forage from the forest was not enough to sustain him. He would die if he did not do something; he must go to the Grovi and offer himself to their mercy. His only hope was that his lifelong friendship with Brak would save his life.

He had to leave as soon as possible, before the snow became too deep and he became too weak to climb the ridge. But first there was something he would have to do. Taking his spear and his axe he went into the forest and cut away a long branch, as long as three times his height. Taking it back to his round-house to work on it in the open doorway, he used his axe to trim the branch until it was smooth, then used his flint knife to cut away at each end in turn until there was a sharp point at both ends. It was dark before he had finished, so he resolved to make this night the last in his camp, possibly the last night of his life.

In the morning he dressed in his warmest clothing, over which he wore his shaman's robes with his mask hanging from one shoulder. He felt that his days must surely now be numbered and he would rather face the coming trials as a shaman, a shaman without a tribe. Then he spent some time in a clearing, hefting what he called his wolf-spear, spinning it around and jabbing it at imaginary attackers. Before he tired himself too much, he placed his knife and his axe in his belt, and carrying his spear and his wolf-spear in each hand, set off to climb the ridge. The first snowfall had not been too heavy, so there were clear patches between the trees, but as he left the trees behind the snow lay all around, causing him to slip and stumble, especially on his weak leg. It took him until the afternoon to reach the top of the ridge. To regain some strength, he sat behind the rocks where he had first met Brak, drank water from an animal bladder, chewed on some dried mushrooms and then lay down on the snow to rest for a while. He was too nervous to sleep, opening his eyes every few seconds to look about.

It had been many years since he had first met Brak here and he missed his friend. He looked forward to seeing him again, even if it could cost him his life. It was time to go again before the light began to fade. He pushed himself up using his spear, then picked up the wolf-spear and left the ridge to start the descent into the valley of the Grovi. He could see down below, just above the tree-line, a small dark shape in the snow. He stopped and peered at it but it was not moving. If he continued on his chosen path it would take him towards this strange thing. He wondered if he should stay high and move further down the valley before descending further, but he was curious as to what it might be. If it was a dead animal, perhaps he could use it for food.

He was a long spear-throw away when it moved and he suddenly realised what this thing was and cursed himself for his curiosity. It was a wolverine, less than half the size of a wolf, but Rat knew that it was powerful and ferocious enough to kill a bear or challenge a pack of wolves. He would rather face any creature than this one. It was standing now, facing him on its four powerful legs, he could see that it was brown with a mask of paler fur that ran across the top of its face. Its ears were pulled back to its skull and he could see that it was sniffing the air to see what he was. He stood totally still, and in the stillness he could feel his heart pounding in his chest. He was not a hunter, and although he had practised throwing spears the other boys had always laughed at his weak and poorly aimed throws. They both remained still for what seemed a long time, he wanted so much to move, perhaps if he took short backward steps this animal would leave him alone and they both could yet live.

Still neither moved, until Rat could stand it no

longer; feeling slowly with his good leg he took a small step back. The wolverine did not move, so he moved a further step backwards, now with his weak leg, but the snow caused him to wobble slightly. Then the wolverine made up its mind, it charged him. It was covering the ground at speed as Rat raised his spear above his head, made himself wait until the creature was close, then threw it with all his strength. The spear missed and fell behind the wolverine. He lowered his long wolf-spear, pointing it straight at the animal, but it leapt above the point and scrabbled along the shaft of the spear trying to reach his body. The weight of the creature landing on the spear was so great that he could not hold it, he dropped the spear and the wolverine dropped with it, rolling in a bundle across the snow. It was now behind him, he swivelled and for a moment, as he drew the axe from his belt, he looked down into its face and saw the jaws were wide and full of savage looking teeth. With all of his strength he brought his axe down onto the animal's head, temporarily knocking it senseless as the axe bounced out of his hand. As the creature fell he reached down and back for the wolf-spear and brought it around his body. The wolverine's eyes opened and it was trying to stand when Rat, now holding the spear with both hands, drove the point deep into its chest. Even as it died its jaws locked onto the shaft of the spear and held it while its body thrashed about, before at last becoming still.

Rat fell panting to his knees and stayed there looking in wonder and relief at what he had just killed. Very few hunters, not even Brak, had achieved what he had just done. For a moment he felt very pleased with himself and regretted that there had not been someone else there to see the fight and praise him afterwards. He had to use the blade of his knife to release the teeth of the creature from the shaft of the wolf-spear. He placed one hand over the heart of the wolverine and said a prayer for its soul, then praised it to make it happy in the next world.

'You were the greatest of warriors; there is no shame in your losing this battle, go in peace.'

He wanted to carry its body to present it to the Grovi but it was too heavy for him, he could not even lift it from the ground. So he skinned the creature as proof of his kill, cutting out its heart and liver, along with strips of flesh sliced from the body. Wrapping the skin around the meat, he hefted it under one arm, then left the remains behind as he limped onwards and down through the forest to the camp of the Grovi below.

7

OLD BONDS

Rat approached the camp of the Grovi using a well worn path that he had travelled along so many times before, he was wary. Even at some distance he expected to smell the fires burning in the long-house, but he could not smell anything. He did not meet anyone on the path. When he reached the outskirts of the camp he stopped and looked to see signs of activity, children playing or some sign of movement, but there was nothing, only silence. It was then that he noticed that the snow all around the camp was laid evenly, without a single footprint to be seen. He placed the remains of the wolverine by a tree, and although he had planned to lay down his weapons when he reached the camp, he thought it best to leave only the heavy wolf-spear and keep his spear and his axe.

He stepped onto the unbroken snow in the clearing that contained the long-house and walked past the twisted tusk of the sea monster. With despair he realised that the Grovi had also left their valley, there was no food to be had here, he was the last man left in the north. Even if they had taken his life he had longed to see the Grovi again: any human company was better than this desolation. Despite Brak's hatred of him, he still cared deeply for the man and was sorry that he would never see him again.

Brak was sitting on his bed, his head in his hands, cold, starving and alone, when he heard the sound of snow crunching outside of the long-house. No animal would make a sound so loud, it had to be a human. He remembered the time when the old ones were slaughtered while the tribe were away at the summer camp and wondered if one of those killers now stood on the other side of the door. He reached for his spear and raising it stood facing the door. It banged back and he saw the blurred figure of a man in the doorway. He shouted, hoping his fear could not be heard in his voice.

'Speak stranger, or you will have this spear stuck in your chest.'

Back came a voice in his own language, a voice he recognised.

'You are even uglier now than I remembered and you were born ugly. If you are going to throw that spear then you best do it now, before that skinny old arm becomes too tired, it is already shaking.'

Rat thought how very old Brak looked now and so frail. For the first time in his life he felt stronger and more powerful than this great chief and warrior. After all, he had just killed a wolverine.

'Rat, is that you?'

'Don't you recognise me, have I changed so much?'

'My sight has almost gone but it is you alright. Did your tribe leave you behind as well, you scheming piece of shit?'

Brak lowered his spear and sat back down with a low groan, then lay back on his bed of furs. Rat came forward and stood over him, Brak was facing away and he could see a deep cut at the side of Brak's neck that disappeared under his beard. There was caked blood on the side of his neck.

'Well, at least my tribe did not try to cut *my* throat before they left me.'

Brak's hands went up to his throat.

'Ah this, well I fell over a root in the forest and landed on a sharp rock, it is nothing.'

'If you say so,' said Rat. 'Do you want to kill me now for coming into your valley, as you warned you would, or will you let me tell you that I did not take Trovi from you, how I saved his life twice, how I took care for him in the tribe and saw that he did well. He has a Salar woman now and you have another grandson. Shall we continue this feud until we both freeze to death or die of starvation?'

He sat down gently on the bed.

'I fear we are both going to die before this winter is over, but for now I would wish to light a fire and share a meal with you before that time comes. Say that you forgive me you obstinate old man.'

Brak's voice was hoarse as he croaked,

'I have no wood, or food, or water.'

'Lay there and rest then, I will see if I can do something about this.'

He stood up to leave, then turned to say something to Brak but saw that his eyes were closed and that his mouth gaped open. He hobbled back to him as quietly as he could and leant over and placed his ear by Brak's mouth, fearing that he had died, but no, he was still breathing. Rat looked about at the deserted long-house with gaps in the walls where Brak had cut away the wooden supports for firewood and remembered how it was when they both were young.

This place had been everything, the core and heart of the tribe, never entirely quiet and still, even during the long winter nights. There was laughter, there were arguments and men being scolded by their women, there were children running around and getting into places where they should not be. There were hearths with lit fires on both sides down the length of the long-house, it was smoky and warm and smelled of the people and the cooking of food. He looked back at Brak who was still asleep, then went quietly out of the door and made his way to the forest.

When he was deep into the forest he dug up garlic bulbs and collected herbs. Using his knife he stripped bark from some green branches and laid them out in strips, then he collected fallen branches, broke them to length and made a bundle bound together with the bark strips. It was a struggle getting back to the long-house with the heavy bundle on his back, but he had done this many times before as a part of his childish chores, so it came back to him well enough. He entered the long-house as quietly as he could and saw that Brak was still asleep. He made up a mound of branches on the hearth, found Brak's fire stones and, after much striking, finally got a spark going that he fanned into a fire. When he was sure that it was going to stay alight he took a large leather vessel and went down to the river to collect water. It was so heavy that he had to heft it onto his shoulder, where it banged against his head each time he stepped forward on his weak leg.

Upon returning to the hearth he dropped hot stones from the fire into the vessel to heat the water. Once more he went out, picking up the wolverine skin and meat he returned to the long-house. Unrolling the skin, he cut up the meat and the offal and cooked them over the fire before filling two bowls with the hot water, dropping in the cooked meat and adding the garlic and the herbs. The skin of the wolverine gave off a dreadful odour so he took it back outside. Only then did he relax, he was exhausted, but seeing Brak again made him happy and he sat there awhile smiling into the fire.

When Brak woke he saw the red glow of the fire flickering on the ceiling of the long-house. He turned his head and saw that Rat sat by the fire stirring a pot. Rat turned to him smiling.

'You ready to eat then? It is a broth so you can drink and eat at the same time, come on sit up.'

Brak sat up with a struggle and sat there slumped in resignation. Rat tipped some meat and broth into a bowl and brought it to Brak.

'Here, get this down you, you will feel a lot better when you have had it.'

Brak took the bowl into his lap and looked up at him.

'What is it, are you going to use your shaman's tricks to poison me eh?'

'I have no need to poison you, if you don't eat that you will be dead by tomorrow.'

He picked up the bowl and thrust it at Brak's face.

'See, it is just meat and broth.'

Then he put the bowl back down into his lap.

'Eat it now.'

Pulling a face, Brak sipped the broth then pulled out a piece of meat and started chewing. He stopped chewing and looked at Rat, then he spat the meat back into the bowl.

'In all my years this is the worst meat I ever put in my mouth.'

Rat seized the bowl from him and picking out a large piece of meat thrust it into his own mouth.

'See, there is nothing wrong with it.'

Then he tasted it and almost retched, it was awful. He could not let Brak see his disgust and chewed on until he could swallow it. He smiled as if he had just eaten the choicest piece of meat, then thrust the bowl back into Brak's lap. He pointed at the bowl and with all the authority he could find shouted,

'Eat it!'

Brak sat there for a few moments holding the bowl, then once more thrust a hand in and pulled out another piece of meat and chewed it with a face contorted with disgust. This time he swallowed the meat, drank more of the broth and continued to eat the whole bowl. Rat was relieved. He filled a bowl for himself, for he too would die if he did not eat, and forced his own meal down. Sitting there now with an empty bowl Brak said,

'Well that tasted liked a wolf's arse, is that what it was?'

Rat stood and started towards the door.

'I'll show you.'

He returned with the skin of the wolverine and unrolled it before Brak.

'This is what you have been eating.'

He stood back with some pride. Brak peered short-sightedly at the skin, then realised what the creature was.

'What, you found this dead? That would account for its foul taste.'

'Oh it was very much not dead when we met, it planned to have me for a meal but now we have eaten it. Here have some more, you need to keep eating and this is all we have for now.'

He refilled Brak's bowl and then his own. Brak sat quietly for a while slowly chewing his meat.

'You killed this? A creature that even I have not been able to kill, yet you killed it?'

'The Earth Mother must have been watching over me,' he said, trying to appear modest and to save Brak's feelings. 'And I was lucky.'

Brak sat and ruminated on this, neither spoke for a while as they drank the broth and chewed their meat. Brak offered the empty bowl to Rat then lay back down on his bed.

'Take that stinking skin out of here, its smell reminds me of that disgusting meat.'

Rat took it outside then returned to sit by the fire. Brak spoke while looking up at the ceiling.

'So, you are a great hunter now, as well as a killer of men.'

Brak had always been repulsed that the Salar sacrificed humans and found it hard to imagine his normally gentle friend as an executioner.

'You said that you had saved my Trovi's life twice, were your tribe going to sacrifice him to your goddess?'

'There was talk of it yes, to ask that she give us warm dry summers again.'

'And did you murder some other innocent in his place, and what good did your goddess do for your tribe after, where were the warm dry summers that he died for?'

'Yes, another man had that honour and I took him to be with the Earth Mother. We can only ask, it is for her to decide if she will give. We had to try.'

'The killing of men for no good reason, that is what separates the Grovi and the Salar. We would kill any man that attacked our tribe, but the Grovi do not kill men without good cause.'

Rat sat for a while, not responding. With his elbows on his knees and his chin perched on his palms he gazed into the fire. Then in a quiet voice, almost a whisper,

'Do you remember when I used to come to your tribe? I would often spend time with your old people, both the men and the women. I was seeking wisdom, anything that would help me become a shaman and I learned many things from your people. I spent most of my time with Deron, your storyteller and keeper of the tribe's history. Well, he told me of the ancient times of your tribe and how they came to this valley and what they found here.'

Brak said nothing but raised his eyebrows for Rat to go on.

'They found another race of humans, not like the Grovi or like the Salar, but they saw that they were doing well in this blessed valley and that they were happy. These people were good to your ancestors and gave them food and shelter. In return your ancestors slaughtered them all, all of the men, all of the women and all of the children.'

He paused and looked to see if there was any reaction from Brak but his face was blank.

'When no one was left alive they used their shelters to live in until this long-house could be built, and ever since the Grovi have lived a good life here, a life that they stole from those innocent ones.'

Brak sighed and pulled on his beard.

'I was Chief of the Grovi, do you suppose that I had not heard this story before? We have carried that shame all through the years, that is why we do not take the life of a human without good reason, we must make amends for the deeds of our ancestors.'

Neither spoke for a while and the only sound was the crackling of the fire. Then Brak spoke in a weary voice,

'Enough, I am tired, I will sleep now. If you are staying then make your bed by the hearth and try to keep that fire alight. I do not want any wolves poking their heads through the gaps in the walls tonight.'

And with that he fell immediately to sleep, leaving Rat to tend the fire during their first night together for many years.

8

THE SEA

Brak was the first to awaken the next morning, he lay there and looked at Rat curled up on furs in front of the fire. Much as he had hated him these past years, he wondered now if he had misjudged his old friend. Perhaps Rat had taken care of Trovi in his new tribe and saved his life, not once but twice. Saving not just Trovi but now Brak himself, coming to him in his final hours with food, fire and water. He saw that he had kept the fire going through the night and that was why he still slept now.

When he had met Rat on the high ridge all those years ago, he had no idea that they would become close friends and that their friendship would form bonds between the tribes that, until finally broken, brought many good things to both races of humans. They shared their skills and weapon making. The Salar excelled at stitching clothes together to make them warm and waterproof; the clothes that Brak wore now were stitched the Salar way. The Grovi were at one with the sea and the Salar learned from them how to take the plentiful food from the shallows of the shore. The Salar crafted better weapons and the Grovi saw this and copied them, but the Grovi knew best how to use those weapons when hunting the great beasts on the plains. Rat was clever and learned quickly, only Rat and Suffi could speak both languages freely. But Brak always wondered how much he could trust him. Once when they were alone he had said to Brak,

'The trouble with the Grovi is that you do not tell lies well. You tell the truth when you could say nothing or say an untruth; you must learn not to show on your face what you are thinking. I just have to look at you to see what you are thinking and that is not good.'

Perhaps to soften his words, Rat had added,

'I prefer you this way, at least you will not surprise me. So let us stay the same. You will tell the truth and I will tell untruths, but hear this Brak and remember, while I tell untruths to others, you are the only person that I do not lie to, I never will.'

Brak had smiled and said,

'Is that promise a lie, how will I ever know? You see where telling falsehoods takes you, no one knows the truth when they hear it. When I speak, everyone knows I am speaking the truth.'

Rat nodded at Brak.

'You will know I am telling you the truth when I tell you what you do not want to hear. I always tell my people what they want to hear but with you I will not, that is my promise.'

Brak never did catch Rat in an untruth, but he knew of many times that the Salar had deceived the Grovi. He lay back down and dozed before he woke again to hear Rat tending the fire. He sat up and watched him bent over the hearth. Rat turned to him, looking him over closely.

'What shall we eat today Brak? We have nothing, if you cannot come up with something and my belly starts to rumble, I may start to think that you are looking like food.'

'I have been thinking, but you will not like what I have to say Rat. You will not want to do this thing.'

He paused and Rat wondered what he was about to

say.

'Do you remember when we were young men and you would come with me to the rocky parts of the shore and you would perch high on a rock while I caught food from the sea?'

Rat remembered very well. In his memory, they were always warm days when the sea was calm and flat. Brak would wait until the sea was at low tide, then he would take off his clothes and wade in the rock-pools, feeling under rocks for crabs, or if he was lucky, catch a fish left behind by the sea. Sometimes he would stand up shouting in pain if a crab had taken hold of one of his fingers. He showed Rat how they could hunt for long shellfish buried in the sand, by looking for the entrance to their burrows then jabbing a bulrush stem, cut with a barb at one end, deep into the sand and pulling out what was a favourite food of the tribe. He would prise limpets from their place with his knife and pull strands of large gleaming black mussels from the rocks. Sometimes he would swim out to rocks that were further out to get the best of them, while Rat sat on a high rock and watched in wonder at his friend's skill. Where the water was deeper, he would often dive down to explore the bottom, pulling back small rocks and feeling under large ones to see what they might be hiding. When he was close to the surface, Rat could see the fine red hairs on his body wafting backwards and forwards as he swam, the way that seaweed swirls around a rock.

'I remember, but what can you take from the sea now that the snows are here?'

'Not me Rat, but you. You will take from the sea this time and then we can eat this day at least.'

'I cannot swim, you know that I am frightened of the sea. It wants to kill me.'

'You can reach what we need from the rocks, you will not be swimming. If I come with you and tell you what must be done, will you do this so we can eat?'

He searched around his bedding and found a sack from which he pulled out assorted sea-shells. Picking out a limpet shell and a mussel shell he held them up to Rat.

'These are what we must find today. We are lucky,

as the moon was almost full last night, so the sea will be low now and make it easier for you, come let us go.'

Rat did not wish to do this, he had never entered the sea. Even when the salmon came into the river, he would not wade in to help with the catching. He had always suspected that water was seeking to take hold of him and drown him, so he had stayed as far away from it as possible all his life. But he knew that they must eat today and there was now no food left. It would have to be done and he felt sure that he could trust Brak to keep him safe. He sighed in resignation, then committed himself.

'I will do it, so come prepare yourself. Wear your warmest clothes and drink this before we go.'

He handed Brak a bowl of boiled water and herbs to warm him from the inside. He then put on all of his warmest clothes but left aside his shaman's robes. He helped Brak into his clothes, handed him his axe, then pulled him to his feet before sliding his own knife and his axe into his belt. Brak rummaged around his bed and found some loosely woven sacks to take with them.

'Come on Brak, keep close to my back so that you do not lose sight of me.'

Brak was feeling stronger now that he had eaten, and was looking forward to going down to the sea where he knew that he would feel renewed. He would once more breathe in the smells that he loved. Rat poked his head out from the doorway and looked around to make sure that it was safe for them to start their journey down the valley. He tugged Brak's arm.

'Let us go now, before I change my mind.'

The sun was shining strongly but the snow still lay all around. Rat looked for wolf tracks and was relieved to see that there were none. He hobbled down to the river bank, often looking over his shoulder to see that Brak was still behind him, then followed the river down to the beach. They rested there for a while, then Brak pointed to where he knew that the beach stopped and the shore became rocky.

'That is where we must go.'

So together they went, Rat hobbling at the front and

Brak walking behind with his eyes fixed on Rat's back; they left the only tracks across the golden sand. There was no life to be seen at the water's edge, apart from two crows that perched on the branches of a washed-up dead tree. Murmuring to each other, they watched with black beady eyes as the men passed. Brak knew that the seals were now far out to sea and that the crabs had left the seashore, heading down to deep water for the winter. Even the razor-shells were now buried too deeply in the sand to be reached with a stick, only limpets and mussels were still here for the taking.

When they reached the rocks, Brak showed Rat how to wade into the shallow pools and take a limpet by quickly sliding his knife between the limpet and the rock before it could clamp down and become almost immovable. At first Rat complained about the cold water, but as he filled the sack tied around his neck he soon forgot he was cold and concentrated on his task. After he had filled two sacks with limpets, Brak told him that in order to collect the largest mussels they would have to walk further out to where the rocks met the deep sea. It was difficult going, so Rat took Brak by his wrist, both to support himself and to guide Brak. Together, they stumbled and fell further and further out on the rocks. Brak warned Rat that he must check behind them at all times, in case the sea came rushing back into the shore to cut them off from escape while so far out. Finally, they reached the outermost edge where the rocks plunged into the sea depths; here they both lay down and reached into the sea to pull up the mussels that hung there in heavy strands.

They were doing well and had filled two more sacks, when Rat overreached himself and slid headfirst into the sea. It was a terrible shock. He came gasping back to the surface and turned to the rock to hold on with cold fingers, his was face just above the water but the sea was pushing his body under the rocky ledge, preventing him from pulling himself up. If he let go he would be swept under the ledge and drown. The cold numbed him and took away his breath and he could feel that his fingers were weakening their hold on the sharp slippery rock. He tried to breathe but the sea was slapping against the back of his head, trying to push his face under the surface. As he had always known, the sea would kill him if it could. He threw his head back to gasp for air and could see the bright blue sky high above, taunting him as he was being pulled down. Water slapped over his face and he choked as he swallowed the salt water. As his hands started to slip off the rock, his head slipped under the surface; looking down with open eyes, he could see the green depths turning to black below him.

Then his wrists were seized with a powerful grip which held him there until the next surge of water pushed his body up, then he could feel his body being lifted out of the sea and dragged painfully over the jagged edge of the rocks. He lay there face down, struggling for breath and staring wide-eyed at the green weed that covered the rock. Brak bent over him and spoke in his ear.

'Come, we must leave straightaway, you will soon be too cold to move and the tide is coming in, pull yourself together, come on, up on your feet.'

Rat wished to lie there for a long time but he understood that they must get moving at once. He took Brak's offered hand and stood, Brak loaded two sacks around his shoulders, then hefted the remaining two around his own. Walking side by side, with their arms around each other's waists, they started on their difficult journey back to the beach. Once there, Rat asked that they stop for a while but Brak insisted that they keep moving in case Rat succumbed to the cold in his wet clothes. Soaring high above them was a sea-eagle, it saw movement on the beach and flew lower to see what this thing might be; it was two humans moving jerkily together as one. The eagle knew that these oddly moving creatures were the only humans it had seen in all the lands that it flew over. It would be worth flying this way again soon to look for carrion.

They were weary when they entered the long-house once more, but Brak would not let Rat rest yet. He made him strip and then covered him with as many furs as he could find before getting the fire going again. Rat shivered for some time, eventually falling asleep while listening to Brak bustling around and to the crackle of the fire. When Rat awoke it was night and he felt warm and secure in the furs. He opened his eyes and saw that his clothes were drying by the fire and that Brak was watching him from his bed. They looked at each other for a while, then Rat said,

'I owe my life to you, I was about to drown when you caught me. You are stronger than you look my friend to lift me so easily.'

'Oh, I did not lift you easily, it took all of my strength but I thought you were a fish worth pulling from the sea. Are you ready to eat and find once again that I am a better cook than you?'

Rat had to agree that the meal of mussels and limpets was very good, although he was not fond of the smell that reminded him of that awful place, the sea, where death always seemed so close. They were full when they both finally lay back on their beds, and in the silence that fell over the long-house, just above the noise of the fire, could be heard the rumbling and gurgling of stomachs. As they slept, the moon that had created the low tide now shone bright over the camp, bathing everything in a spectral light. Silently appearing from the forest, a snow leopard slowly looked around, taking everything in, listening intently and sniffing deeply of all the scents. She made her way down one side of the long-house; coming to a gap in the wall she peered in, seeing the flickering light of the low fire and smelling the shellfish within. She thrust her head fully inside and looked around, when she saw the men asleep in their beds her eyes came to sharp focus. Her mouth was open and she panted slightly from the stress of being so close to humans.

Withdrawing her head, she made her way further around until by the door she found the wolverine pelt. She was curious but the smell repelled her, she coughed quietly and backed away from it. Turning away, she padded over to the twisted horn standing in the centre of the camp, where she circled around it before rubbing herself against it with the length of her body. Suddenly, she launched her body upright and laid her paws near the top of the horn, unsheathing her claws she scraped them down its full length. Sitting, she looked haughtily around the camp as if she were now its ruler and the camp had been added to her wide domain. Satisfied, she stood then vanished ghostlike into the forest. Clouds moved across the face of the moon and snow began to fall. Snowflake by snowflake the tracks of the snow leopard filled and were soon no more.

9

DAYS OF THE MAMMOTHS

'I need a shit.'

Rat opened his eyes and looked over at Brak sitting on his bed.

'I need to take a shit,' he said, looking directly at Rat.

Rat threw back his furs and sat up.

'Feel free friend. On your way, go and take your shit.'

'Well I would, but the last time that I spent any time out there alone, that dark bitch-wolf..'

'Roden?'

'If that is what you call her, she tried to kiss me on the lips. If I go out there alone for a shit, I may turn around and find her sniffing my arse.'

Rat smiled.

'Come on then, we will collect wood while we are out.'

Taking their weapons, they went into the forest and Brak did what he needed to do while Rat watched from a distance. When he had finished, Brak wiped himself with snow, pulling a face at its coldness.

Rat laughed to see his friend so discomfited.

'Went it well then, the shit?'

Brak was rather grumpy when he replied.

'As shits go, yes. I have not had one in a long time, if you do not eat you do not need to take a shit.'

Rat collected herbs and then together they rolled two bundles of branches so that they could carry them back to the long-house. Although Brak would never say so out loud, he found it amusing following behind his friend, watching the shouldered bundle bouncing from side to side as Rat struggled to walk with the heavy load on his weak leg. He could not help but admire this man who had made a good life for himself in this harsh world while being so crippled. They dropped the bundles by the fire, Rat brewed them a hot drink and they settled down for a quiet day. Brak was happy that they had enough shellfish left to feed them well tonight and they would worry where more food would come from tomorrow. Rat wondered if Brak's mood might be improved if he were encouraged to talk.

'What say you that today I will listen while you tell me stories of the summer-hunting on the plains?'

Although Rat had heard the stories many times before, he had never shared those days with his friend or his tribe, so he never tired to hear the about the hunting of the bison and the mammoths.

'And then afterwards, this night, I wish to visit the land of the Earth Mother if you will watch over me.'

Brak nodded.

'I would do that.'

Brak sat on his bed preparing his story while Rat built up the fire. When they both felt ready, Rat lay back on his bed with his head propped up on one hand. Brak tried to cross his legs underneath himself, but failing, sat normally.

'I will tell you the story of one summer when I was a young man and killed many beasts that summer on the plains and took Culu to be my woman. Have I told you of this before?'

'No, never,' lied Rat.

'Well,' he said, stroking his beard as he always did while telling stories, 'back then the summers were always long and filled with sunshine. We set off early one morning and met your tribe on the high mountain ridge to go down together onto the plains. Everyone was happy, there was singing and chanting as we trekked, even though we were laden down with weapons and food. We could not speak with the Salar as you can speak with us, but we could make ourselves understood well enough. I always missed you during those summers but I could make friends of sorts with the men of your tribe.' He smiled ruefully. 'Not that I trusted any of them.'

'It takes three days to march to the plains, four to come back with the meat, furs and bones. Well, three days later saw us at the camp where we dug up the yurts and, if needed, repaired them. I stayed in my family's yurt; it always felt strange to be sleeping without the tribe around me. The first day we would erect the yurts and on that night we would eat the food that we had brought and visit one another's campfires. Now here is a strange thing,' he paused for dramatic effect. 'There is no wood on the plains.' His eyes widened in mock surprise. 'So what do you suppose we would do for a fire, mmm?'

Rat, who knew the answer well enough, said,

'No wood, nothing? What could you use?'

'Dung,' said Brak slapping his thighs. 'Dung, there is mounds of the stuff on the plains and it burns well enough, does dung.'

'Ah, dung, interesting but tell me how you won Culu.'

'I went to her family's yurt every night and took them food. They were impressed with my hunting stories, Culu especially, so I did not wait long to ask her family if she could stay with me in our family yurt. And so it was. We were together from that day. One day soon after, I took her to walk with me so that we could be alone, well you might guess why, eh? Well, when we were far away from the camp I lay down in the long grass and called for her to join me, but before she could I felt pain all over my face and my legs and my arms, guess what I had laid down upon.'

With raised eyebrows he held his arms wide and lifted his palms to make Rat reply.

'Ants,' thought Rat. 'I have no idea, what was attacking you?'

'Ants,' laughed Brak, 'I had lain down on an ant's nest; I ran around and around while Culu tried to catch up with me and brush them off.'

He chuckled to himself at the memory and in the same instant felt the loss of the woman and of the time when he was young and in love. He fell quiet and looked at the floor for a while remembering. Rat guessed what was going through his mind and when Brak looked up again, he saw by the sadness on Brak's face that he was right. He would give him time to recover.

'Well Brak, we never will lie with a woman again,

will we? I cannot say that it bothers me so much now, but I do miss having a woman's body to hold in the night, even if their cold feet suck the warmth from the bed.'

He smiled encouragement to Brak, who cleared his throat and continued with his story.

'Let us talk of the hunting, great times.'

Rat could hear a change in his voice, quieter and with a slight tremor to it. There was a pause then Brak pulled himself together, swallowed and continued once more in his usual strong voice. But Brak, being Brak, still showed some of the pain on his face. He told first of the hunting of the bison, who came to the plains in such numbers that they could be seen in all directions, as far as the eye could see.

'It takes two men Rat. Two men bent over and covered in hides, with the man in front holding a set of horns so that you look and smell like the rest of the herd. That way you get up really close to them, and when you get so close you can hear them chewing the grass, you throw down the hides and in one move bring up your hunting spear to throw it at the nearest one.'

He stood up, first holding then throwing an imaginary spear.

'If you are lucky, the two men can kill two beasts.'

He sat down again, smiling at the memory.

Rat thought to amuse Brak.

'Is that not dangerous for the man at the back, if a male comes around and takes an interest in mounting this false beast?'

But Brak just stared at him as if he was mad, talking nonsense, this hunting was a serious matter and not to be made light of. When he felt that his rebuking stare had done its work, he continued with his story.

'Ah, the food we would eat at night: first was the stomach contents, delicious, then all the meat you could eat until your belly felt it was going to burst. The juices would run down your chin and drip onto your chest. You only ever got to eat the strips of dried meat that we brought back at summer's end, it was not the same Rat, not the same. What I would not give to eat some of that meat now.'

He lay back on his bed and thought about the meat, his stomach rumbling loudly enough for Rat to hear.

Rat said nothing but set about tending the fire. He knew that Brak would talk again when he was ready. He thought on how much of life he had missed during those wonderful times on the plains, and how he had never known what it was like to share the friendship and dangers of a hunt. Instead, every year he had been left behind with Sabal and the old ones. For a young man, it was a frustrating time and a loss of face that had to be re-earned every year when the tribe returned laden with meat and mammoth bones at the summer's end. The men would sit chattering excitedly at night about their great exploits, while he could only sit in silence and nod and smile at their stories.

After they had both had time to themselves and their thoughts, they resumed their positions and Brak began his story of the killing of the mammoths. Although the migrating bison passed across the plains and could only be hunted for a week or two, the mammoths were always to be found moving around somewhere on the grasslands.

'Rat, you have not seen these beasts, you have seen their bones but to see such a creature walking across the plains, well it takes your breath away. We had long ago found that they were difficult to kill with our spears, we could bring one down eventually but men were often killed. They run so fast, faster than we can run, you cannot outrun them when they charge, and when they come for you, you can feel the ground shake beneath you. Every man is frightened on those hunts. That is why we usually killed the young ones; you need only to cripple one to stop it from being able to follow its mother, and eventually it will be yours for the taking.

It was easier when the Salar joined us on the hunts. Your tribe would wait ahead of the herd, for when these beasts see and smell enemies they group together, with the bulls and the old females at the front to defend the young ones. That was when we would rise up from where we were hidden in the long grass and attack the young ones at the back of the herd. It was still very dangerous and sometimes we lost men, but if you could put your spears into the legs of the young ones, stop them from walking, they would be left behind with only their mothers to protect them.'

He paused, remembering.

'When the herd moved on we would wait, the two tribes, and watch the mothers with their crippled young. Some mothers would not wait for long before they left their young but many would wait until the young one would die, even then sometimes staying to sniff and nudge the body and try to bring it back to life. We would wait as long as it took; if a young one were still alive when its mother left we would kill it quickly, watching all the while to make sure that the mother did not return. We became very skilled at this and no young ones would survive their passage over the plains, we fed so well during those days.'

He looked proudly at Rat. Rat looked at Brak and said nothing. Brak could tell by his look that he wanted to speak and was thinking how he would say his thoughts.

'I hope that my words do not make you feel badly that you were not there. I was only wanting for you to understand how wonderful those hunts were.'

Rat still kept his peace, he sighed then lay back on his bed staring at the roof timbers. Brak fell silent, he must have upset his friend in some way. Time passed in silence. Then Rat sat up and spoke.

'Those creatures are all but gone and I hear that only the very old ones still travel over the plains, there are no young ones now. Consider this Brak, if you kill all of the young ones where will the new adults come from? Your tribe and mine have destroyed them all. Did you not think that by killing the young, you were killing your own future time on the plains?'

Brak did not welcome being spoken to like this. A part of him knew that Rat was speaking the truth and he resented it.

'There were so many in the old days, their numbers covered the plains and their mounds of bones told us that they had lived there from days long before we came to these valleys. How could we, so weak compared to them bring them to their knees? We never thought that possible. Then when the young became scarce, they were valued ever more highly as a prize and the greater the honour to the hunter that killed one. I took pride in those last kills.'

Rat shook his lowered head.

'You were a fool Brak. You were all fools.'

Brak was hurt and angry. He was hurt because he was proud of his stories and had wanted to make Rat happy with his tales, after all Rat had asked to hear them. He was angry because he knew that even Rat had been aware what had happened to the mammoths and why they were now just a ghostly herd of the old ones. Rat looked up at Brak and spoke strongly but sorrowfully.

'I was the tribe's Shaman, I spoke for the Earth Mother, and when I knew what you were doing to those beasts I spoke with our Chief, Dalkan, and told him that some young must be spared. His words to me were that if he did not hunt them, the Grovi would and the Salar would look foolish and weak, he would not stop.'

Brak became exasperated.

'But he was right. It has always been our way to take what we want, and when there is no more, well, we move on to fresh valleys and plains and take again, it is our way and we, our two tribes, have done well have we not? There is always more to be found in new lands.'

'Brak, there may be no new lands to find, our tribes are even now heading south to the old valleys where the game may no longer be plentiful. We must respect the Earth Mother or she will no longer care for us.'

'The Grovi have no Earth Mother but I understand you; it is what it is. In any case, we are no longer part of this. You and I are like the last of the giant beasts, we old ones must carry on without our children.'

Rat had anger in his voice.

'No, we are not like those cursed creatures, most of our young ones still walk the earth. Yes we are old and may die soon, but our tribes will live on while their herds will cease to exist, that is the difference.'

Brak spoke sternly, his manner becoming chief-like.

'Enough, enough,' he waved his hands in dismissal, 'I will not fall out with you over this. We should eat, it is your turn to cook the meal. I will sleep; wake me when it is ready.'

And with that he lay down and turned his back to Rat; laying there with open eyes, not sleeping but feeling angry and frustrated. Rat started preparing to cook the meal, it was a fiddly business shelling and cleaning the shellfish. He vented his anger by being noisy and banging and throwing items about. The shadow that had been cast in the room was not just that they had fallen out over the hunting, but in the realisation that conjuring up past glories had brought home to them both what they were now, old and alone, without their tribes and families. When the meal was cooked, Rat put some in a bowl and shook Brak's shoulder.

'Here, your meal is ready. Not as good as when you prepared it but edible all the same.'

Brak, whose anger had subsided, pretended to wake from a deep sleep, stretching and yawning, he sat up. He took the bowl and joined Rat in eating the last of their food. Hoping to put their argument behind them, he thought to compliment his friend.

'It is good, really, very good, you are learning Rat.'

Rat gave a mock bow.

'Well thank you Chief, I am humbled by your words.'

Brak stiffened, was Rat now mocking him? But he knew that he must not to react as he would have done as a young chief, with anger. A part of him was aware that his friend was only trying to ease the atmosphere with humour; he must fight to see it that way and not let his pride spoil their friendship. He decided to play the game that Rat had started. Being as chief-like as he could, he said,

'You are not pleasing your Chief and you smell of fish; your appearance is wretched and you have no manners. You insult my sight. Take the shells down to the midden and throw them in, then throw your ugly self in after.'

Rat bowed and picking up the opened shells and other scraps, he bowed once again.

'Thank you my Chief, you are kind to me.'

Then he walked out as humbly as he could. Once outside he grinned to himself, they were friends once more and he was to visit the land of the Earth Mother this coming night.

When he returned he set about preparing the herbs and mushrooms that he would need when night fell. It was important to get the portions exactly right, too much of one or two ingredients and he would not return from his trip back to his body, trapped forever in the other world. He heated the plant materials until they were dry, ground them between two rocks then added the powder to hot water and boiled the mixture over the fire. When he was satisfied it was ready, he removed the bowl from the fire and placed it to one side to allow it to cool. Brak lay on his side on his bed, watching him but saying nothing.

Just in case he did not return, he decided to pray and chant now, so that his last deeds would gain favour with the Earth Mother. He dressed in his shaman's cloak and jewellery, then painted his face with pigments; totally absorbed in his task, he did not notice that Brak had fallen asleep and was gently snoring. When he looked up and saw that

Brak was sleeping he smiled, he did not need Brak yet, he would let him sleep. He put on his mask and started to pray out loud.

'Bless my friend Brak and allow him to live through this winter, bless my family and tribe on the plains and let them pass south to good lands, where they will be warm and find game in abundance. Bless me, your servant and allow me to visit your land this night and return to my body after. I have nothing to sacrifice, but pledge that if you give Brak and I a creature to eat, I will offer it in sacrifice to you. Please send food to us.'

He then removed his mask, keeping on his robes he lay back and joined Brak in sleep. When they woke it was dark outside and Rat was keen to go ahead with his journey to the spirit world, perhaps there would be some message there that could save them.

'Brak, you promised to watch over me while I passed through to the world of the Earth Mother, are you ready and prepared to do that? If I do not come back then bury my body where the wolves cannot reach it.'

'I am ready, although I do not believe in your god I

hope that you find what you seek, but if I find myself alone I doubt that I will be able bury you deep, the ground is too hard now. You will be the lucky one, for if you die I will not have much time to live. I will be alone with only your corpse for company.'

Rat nodded then stood.

'Let us start this.'

Rat cleared a space in the long-house and drank all of the liquid he had prepared earlier. Then he put on his mask and started to slowly dance. Brak recognised parts of the dance that mimicked the movements of various animals: a wolf, a bison, a mammoth, and finally a bird that was especially sacred to the Salar, the snowy owl. Rat copied the owl's flight in slow motion, starting with the launch from a high tree and the silent steady drop onto a hare. On his knees, he mimicked the death struggles of the hare with his hands, then the tearing of the meat. Rat then slumped sideways into a heap before rolling onto his back. Brak came and sat by his side, he wanted to remove the mask so that he could see the face of his friend, but Rat had warned him not to do this, or to speak to him until he returned. So Brak sat and sang quiet songs to himself while holding the red coral-bead necklace he had once given to Culu.

Rat was in blackness, then falling, falling through clouds. He was flying at a great height along the coast, he glided lower but was still high as he came to a beach. Below, he saw two figures struggling across the sand with their arms around each other's waists and with bags draped across their necks. They were halfway up the beach when a ferocious wind whipped up the sand and drove it knee high onto them, causing them to stumble. The wind became stronger and raised the sand higher than their heads. He could make out that they were bent double under the onslaught before they disappeared beneath the undulating blanket of sand. He circled around and flew up the valley where he could see the sea-monster's tusk in the centre of Brak's camp, a snow leopard sat in the doorway of the long-house staring down the valley. Circling back to the beach, he saw that the wind had dropped and the sand was now still. Only one human shape could be seen face down and half covered in sand. It moved its arms under its chest and raised its upper body ready to stand. Before he could see who it was, everything turned black once more and he gasped as he realised that he was back in his body. Brak heard the gasp and pulled away the mask. His friend looked white and there was fear on his sweating face, his breathing was ragged. He laid his hand on Rat's chest to reassure him and waited for him to recover.

10

SONTY

Rat was not feeling well when they awoke the next morning, his head and his stomach ached. They had no food left and he had no intention of returning to the beach to collect more shellfish, he was now more frightened of the sea than ever. They both lay on their beds in a malaise, and inertia made their limbs feel too heavy to move.

A man came bursting through the doorway and landed in a heap on the floor. Brak and Rat reached for their axes and moved down the long-house to stand over him. He seemed overloaded with furs and weapons. Rolling onto his back, he looked up at them and although his face was rather blurred to Brak, Rat could see that he was young, with a wispy beard, thin and frightened. He looked similar in appearance to Brak and his tribe, so Rat spoke to him in the language of the Grovi.

'Are you alone, are there any more of you outside?'

He understood and spoke back in similar fashion.

'No, there is only me. There were five of us but I am the only one left.'

Pointing at Rat he said,

'Three of us were like you,' then turning to Brak, 'I and another like this man. We were rejects from our tribes and tried to make a living together, but they did not survive and now there is only me. When each died I took some clothing for warmth and so this is how you find me this day. I recognised this long-house as like the one that my tribe lived in, but this camp seemed deserted. I did not expect to find anyone in here; I am so happy that I am no longer alone.'

He looked at them both in turn, smiling in his relief. Rat offered him a hand and he took it to stand.

Brak realised he was replying to Rat in the language of the Grovi and he was delighted to hear someone of his own race speaking. Turning to Rat he said,

'Ask him his name and where he is from.'

Rat looked at him, nonplussed, then Brak realised, feeling foolish, that he could ask him himself, they were of the same race. The young man was bewildered by the conversation but answered directly to Brak.

'I am Sonty and my tribe lived east of here, but these last five years I have been alone, except for the men I met and bonded with. We have had no place to call home in all this time. We would ask tribes to take us in, but when they saw that we were two races, no tribes of either race would have us. Have you any food, I am starving?'

'We do not,' said Rat. 'We ate the last of our food last night, we can give you nothing except a warm drink.'

Sonty replied in the language of the Salar to say,

'I will take that if you will kindly offer it, it is something to fill my belly. Why are you two here alone?'

'Our tribes have left us behind to go south, we are too old to travel far. I, Rat, am crippled in one leg and this man Brak has little sight.'

Brak did not like them speaking in the language of the Salar.

'I am impressed that, like Rat here, you can speak in either tongue, but let us talk only in my speech, then I will understand all that is said. Come, join us at our hearth and Rat will heat up some water and herbs and you can have that until we can find something to eat.'

As they moved back to the hearth, Sonty noticed that, as Rat had said, he limped badly on one leg. He had never seen anyone with an infirmity before, except for the occasional injured hunter. Certainly no child born that way could live to be a man. Rat stoked the fire and set stones to be heated, then ground enough herbs for the three of them. When he had finished he dropped the hot stones into water and added the herbs. Then he poured the hot liquid into bowls and handed them to the two men.

'Here Sonty, see if that helps, for a while at least.'

Sonty, kneeling by Brak's bed, cupped the bowl in his hands and drank. He was very thirsty and the drink would stave off his hunger for a little while. Now that he was so close, Brak could make out the features of his face and was struck by how like his son Trovi he was. While Rat could speak their language well enough, it pleased Brak to hear it spoken properly for the first time since his tribe had left. He patted his bed by the side where he was sitting.

'Here Sonty, sit by me and let us talk.'

Sonty took his bowl with him and sat by Brak, holding it out to Rat for a refill while talking with Brak. They became engrossed in talk, as Brak asked him about his tribe and his life so far, talking fast and in low voices. Rat sat on his bed watching them, feeling cut off from Brak. It was as if he were no longer in the long-house with them. He pursed his lips and thought deeply about what this could mean to him. Not only was this young man coming between him and his friend, he was another mouth to feed when they had no food. He got up and walked up and down the long-house, then he returned and sat on his bed unnoticed by Sonty and Brak. He lay back and watched them. Brak was more animated than Rat had seen since he had reunited with him, and every now and then he gave a throaty chuckle and Sonty would giggle in response.

Finally, Brak became tired and told Sonty that he would rest and that he should go and talk with Rat while he slept. Rat smiled at Sonty and beckoned him over, patting his bed and inviting him to sit by his side. Talking quietly so that Brak could not hear, he nodded towards Brak's prone back.

'A great man that, a great hunter and a great chief, his sight has almost gone now but he is still a rare man. Would that you could be that great one day Sonty eh? If we all make it through this winter together then perhaps you will become a man like him.' He leaned in to him, put his arm around his shoulder and looked him in the eyes. 'A great chief and warrior, how would that be mmm?'

Rat heard Brak's low snore. Still leaning in to Sonty he whispered in the language of the Salar,

'You are welcome here young Sonty but know your place. Brak and I have been friends since we were children, do not come between us. Do you understand eh?'

Sonty whispered back to Rat.

'I do, please do not be cross with me, I mean no

offence.'

'None is taken, so long as we understand one another we will be friends I am sure. Make your bed up by that hearth further down the long-house, then come back to me and we will discuss how we are to eat today.'

Sonty made his bed and collected his weapons in a pile by his hearth, a hearth which had no fire in it and was cold. When he was satisfied that he had made his space comfortable, he went back and sat by Rat, who called out to Brak to wake him.

'Brak, Brak, wake up man.' Brak opened his eyes. 'Come on, wake up we must talk.'

Brak rolled on to his side and looked at them both. For a fleeting moment he seemed confused, as if he did not know who these men in his long-house were.

'What is it that we must talk about?'

'We have nothing to eat, and now that Sonty has joined us we must find something before the day is over.'

Brak and Rat discussed what they might do and Sonty, remembering the warning words of Rat, kept his thoughts to himself and sat in silence. After much talk of what could be done, nothing was suggested that would give them enough for a meal. Silence fell as each man was lost in his own thoughts, desperately seeking for a solution before they starved to death. Finally, Sonty spoke up.

'There is one way of finding food, in the river, I was shown how by my tribe. We can only do this thing once this year in this stretch of the river, but we may find enough to eat for this night, if we are lucky.'

Both Brak and Rat turned to him with interest and demanded to know what they would find in a river that contained no fish in the winter. Sonty reminded them that beneath the rocks of the river, that was now slow flowing and shallow since the snow had fallen, were to be found crayfish. Brak was angry with himself for forgetting that as a small boy he had often caught the family supper that way.

'Of course, of course, when we were children we would gather sacks of them and cook them around the fire at night, a good idea Sonty. I will not even need my sight to help you, just guide me to the river and I'll be happy to feel under the rocks. Rat, bring some sacks, one for each of us, let us go.'

Brak seemed to have come alive again in the company of Sonty and at the thought of getting into water again, even if it would be only knee deep. They took sacks and their axes. The sun was shining and it felt good to be setting off on a hunting journey again. Rat led the way, Brak in the middle and Sonty brought up the rear. The river was not far and soon they were standing on its bank. The bright sunlight sparkled on the ripples, so that the surface seemed to shimmer with light. Brak enjoyed hearing the river again, even when slow moving it had its own music for him. They made their way upriver for quite a way, before going down the bank and experiencing the shock of the freezing cold water moving around their legs. Sonty made his way over to the far shore, Brak stayed by the near shore and Rat took up position in the middle. Slowly they made their way backwards down the river, pulling up rocks and feeling quickly for the crayfish before they could escape. Every now and then one of them would cry out that he had caught one, sometimes holding it up for the others to see before dropping it in his sack.

Their hands soon became numb with the cold and they stopped often to hold them under their armpits to try and get some warmth back into them. It was painful work but Brak was so happy that he sang as he worked, an old fishing song that was known by all of his race, Sonty joined in with him and even Rat hummed along quietly. By the time they had reached the point on the river by their camp they each had a sackful of crayfish.

They were in good spirits as they walked back to the long-house with the sacks over their shoulders. Once there they built up the fire and placed stones to heat; while waiting for the stones to become hot Rat and Sonty went into the forest for herbs and more wood. When the stones were ready, they tipped them into a vessel of water and then threw in some of the crayfish and herbs, before sitting staring into the pot, waiting for the short time that it took for them to turn red. They fed well that night and there were enough crayfish left over to allow some to be stored in the coldest part of the long-house for the next day. With full bellies the old men lay on their beds and Sonty brought some of his bedding to lay between them. He expected a rebuke from Rat but, apart from a hard stare, he said nothing. They all lay in silence for a while, enjoying the warmth from the crackling fire and the satisfaction of full stomachs.

Being in the river today had reminded Brak of the days of autumns past when the salmon would run in the river. After the summer days hunting on the plains, these were also golden times for the tribe, when food was in abundance for all. So many fish would start the run that the whole tribe would enter the river to catch the fish in the shallows, and drying racks would be set up to preserve some fish for the winter. There was safety in numbers from the bears, but even with all of the tribe together, occasionally a large male bear would join them to take the best fishing spots. When that happened, it was best just to relinquish that place and move away until the bear had taken its fill. He remembered a young Trovi holding onto the tail of a fish that was as long as he was, screaming with the pleasure and thrill of it all as he was dragged along the river by the wriggling fish. He could see Culu, with her back to him, standing barefoot and on tiptoe to arrange the filleted fish on the highest branches of the drying racks. The meals, wonderful for the first few weeks, became tiresome when yet another salmon was served up, making him long for the feasts of meat on the plains. He opened his eyes, turned on his side and rested his head on one hand to look at Rat.

'Remember the fish runs Rat, great times eh? Even the last one before my tribe left was something to behold. More fish than a man could eat. Culu would fill one of those fish with herbs, wrap it in grass, then cover it in clay to bake by the fire, wonderful!'

Rat opened his eyes and on the floor Sonty sat up and paid attention.

'I remember them well Brak but, as you know, I have never been a man for getting wet, and everything and everybody reeked of fish for weeks. You could fill your belly well enough but eating fish every day, after a while ugh!'

He pulled a face of disgust. Sonty had been looking at each man as he spoke, he could see that they were close friends who had a deep affection for each other. Brak smilingly said to Rat.

'I think that you came to stay with me and my family when you were a boy so that you would escape your duties during the run of the fish with your own tribe. That way you could watch us at work without feeling guilty, am I right?'

'You are a harsh man Brak, I had not seen you for all of the summer, I was just renewing our friendship.' Then smiling, 'well there may be some truth in what you say.' He waggled his head from side to side, as if weighing up the truth. 'I am much better at watching work than doing it I think. That is why I am a shaman, I am too clever to be a hunter.'

Sonty was not sure if Rat was joking but Brak could see that he was by the way he had cocked one eyebrow in the way that he always did when he was not being serious.

'You are too lazy to be a hunter Rat, you would rather stay in the camp and sniff around the women.'

Sonty wondered why Rat did not defend himself by pointing out that he was crippled and could never have kept up with the hunters.

'If I had chased other women, my first woman, Asa, would have cut my balls off, whereas the second one, Loli, well she would have given me away if she could.'

He fell silent, then.

'I wonder where Loli is now and how my family are doing, are they still on the plains? The snow has not been too heavy here yet, we must hope that they are finding the same.'

Both he and Brak became lost in their thoughts. Long moments passed until Sonty cleared his throat and broke the silence.

'You two have been friends for many years?'

Rat was the first to reply.

'Since we were boys we have played and roamed in the valleys together. My tribe lived in the next valley and since we met we have both known each other's tribes. I spent almost as much time here as I did with my own tribe. When Brak became chief of his tribe, it led to trading and shared hunting. We never went to war with one another, although,' and here he glanced at Brak, 'some years ago Brak and I and the two tribes did fall out, then our tribes left us behind to go south. I came to this camp and found Brak here alone, as grumpy and bad tempered as I remembered him to be. But, alone as we were, we only had each other, so friendship again seemed the better choice for both of us.'

Brak stroked his beard and spoke in a quiet voice.

'Whatever time we have left is time to be shared, for we have lost our families and our tribes and now we only have each other. Well, until you came and joined us Sonty.'

Rat turned his gaze to Sonty and said,

'Tell us how you came to be here and what befell your companions; how they died and yet you still live to sit here with us.'

'I was told to leave by my tribe, and after wandering alone for a long time I was lucky to find the four others, they were kind enough to take me into their group. It was difficult, food was hard to come by, some tribes would give us food before they sent us on our way, but most chased us off with threats that they would kill us if we returned. We could not find enough food, we became weaker and thinner, with no strength to go on. One by one they gave up and let death come to them.'

Rat's eyes were still fixed upon him.

'You are thin boy, but when you came into our long-house you still were very much alive. How so Sonty, why do you still live?'

A look of alarm passed over Sonty's face; Brak was also staring at him, he was not expecting this.

'I cannot lie, one time we tried to carry off some women, but they fought so hard and screamed so loud their men came running and three of my friends were killed. It was only myself and one man, like you Rat, that escaped. He was injured by a spear and the wound became swollen and wept with pus, he died not many days later, leaving me alone again. They did not die of hunger, if I have offended you then I am sorry.'

He looked back and forth at the two men trying to gauge their emotions. Neither Rat nor Brak spoke for some moments, then Brak, looking more solemn than Sonty had seen since he had arrived at the camp spoke.

'We do not suffer such behaviour, that was a bad thing that you did. But it would seem that your companions paid in full, if you survived then so be it. I will accept that and forgive you.'

Sonty was relieved, he looked to Rat, who spoke in a voice that was cold.

'You told us a lie. You have not been honest with us, despite our hospitality. Like Brak, I will forgive you but now I wonder if anything you say is to be trusted.'

'I only told you they died of hunger because I knew that you would be angry with me if I told you the truth. You can trust me now.'

Rat spoke tersely.

'Go, take your bedding back to where I showed you by that hearth and I will shortly bring you a warm drink before we sleep.'

Sonty picked up his bedding and returned to the cold hearth. He lay down with his back to Rat and Brak and pulled the furs around him. Brak raised his eyebrows at Rat then,

'No drink for me Rat, I am tired from the day in the river and will go to sleep now.'

With that, he lay down and was soon snoring. Rat heated some water and rummaged in his bag of herbs to select some special plants that had magical properties. Not for himself but for Sonty. When the drink was prepared, he walked down to where Sonty had his bed.

'Here lad, drink up, this drink will make you feel better and sleep soundly, I promise.'

Sonty turned and sat up to take the proffered bowl. Blowing on the surface to cool it, he then gulped it down. He pulled a face at the bitterness.

'Ugh, that was awful, the worst drink I ever had.'

'Lay back down, you will feel sleepy very soon. Sleep well and I will see you in the morning.'

He took the bowl from Sonty and returned to his

own bed by the hearth. He gazed into the fire and threw some more branches onto it, enough to last the night. When he had gauged that Sonty was asleep, he returned to lay down by his side where he could whisper into his ear. Sonty was dreaming. He was sat against a wall at one end of a deserted long-house, no hearths were lit and the only light was illuminating where he sat, the rest was in darkness. He felt that he was not alone in the long-house, there was someone at the far end in the dark. A voice spoke to him.

'Can you hear me Sonty?'

Sonty felt no fear but knew that he must tell this voice the truth.

'Yes, I can hear you. Who are you?'

'I am the Listener, you must speak in truths. Will you tell me only the truth?'

'I will.'

'When you were rejected by your tribe, how did you live?'

'I befriended a boy who also lived in the wild, there

was no food to be had, we were starving.'

'Go on.'

'When we were both sure to die, I killed the boy and I ate his flesh.'

He put his hands up and covered his face in shame.

'Very good Sonty, you speak the truth well.'

Silence. Then Sonty spoke through his fingers.

'Are you still there Listener?'

'I am here, tell me more.'

'There were other boys and men. I would befriend them and we would try to live, but if we ran out of food I would kill and eat them, it was the only way to survive. I am so sorry, so sorry.'

He started to weep behind his hands but then gathered himself and continued in a faint voice.

'One time there were five of us and three were killed by a tribe for attacking their women. One man survived with me, but he was wounded and died from his wounds. I did not kill him but I ate his flesh.'

'The men you are with now, will you kill them?'

'No I will not, not while we have food, there is no need.' Sonty paused, then, 'but, if we cannot find food and will all starve, I will have no choice but to save myself, though they are good and kindly men.'

'You have spoken truthfully and well Sonty, now go to sleep and I will watch over you, sleep.'

The area around Sonty grew dark and he lay down in the long-house, reassured to know that someone was watching over him. He had spent so many nights alone and terrified in the wilderness. He did not feel alone now, he slept.

In the morning, Rat rose early and went outside to consider what he should do about Sonty. He walked around the camp, coming to the tusk he noticed that there were deep scratches down its surface that ran from near the tip to the base. Turning the corner of the long-house, he looked to where the distant midden pit was and saw the small dark shape of Roden lying still, high up on a slope and looking down on the pit. He returned to the long-house, went to stand by Sonty's bed and tapped him with his foot.

'Wake up lad, we need to get this place tidy. I want you to take the crayfish shells down to the midden.'

Sonty began to protest that he was tired, but Rat quickly knelt down, placed a hand over his mouth and said,

'Quiet young Sonty, we do not want to wake our great Chief do we? Make your way out of the door, and with your back to the sea, in a line from that great tusk, you will find the midden, by the edge of the forest. Go quietly now.'

He removed his hand from Sonty's mouth, and placed it under his elbow to slowly lift him from the floor. Then he handed him a sack containing the shells, nodded towards the door and placed a finger over his own lips to remind Sonty that he must be quiet. Sonty stopped at the door and looked back at Rat who waved him on. Sonty turned back to pick up his axe, but Rat shook his head and spoke in a hoarse whisper,

'You will not need that.'

Sonty held up his hand and stepped out of the long-house. He walked to the tusk and, as instructed, turned his back to the sea and set off towards the forest, following human tracks in the snow that he assumed were Rat's. It took a little time, but then he saw the land fall away into a depression, and as he came closer he saw the snow-covered mounds of shells that had been collected over many generations, along with bones and pieces of hide. Tentatively, he stepped onto the nearest mound of shells and emptied the sack of shells from last night's meal. He felt the pangs of hunger, no doubt they would not be eating the remaining crayfish until tonight. Looking about, he found a bone and put it in his mouth.

Standing and holding the bone with a hand on either end, he grunted and strained to bite through it to see if any marrow remained inside. His eyes were squinted tight shut with the effort, but when the bone would not break he opened them and to his horror saw that standing at the edge of the pit, watching him, was a large dark wolf. He looked over his shoulder to gauge the distance to the long-house, it looked far away. He started to back away, his feet slipping and sliding on the shells. The faster that he backpedalled the more he slipped until, with flailing arms, he fell backwards. Still on his back, he looked between his knees to see where Roden was, she had not moved but continued to watch him, curious to know what this stranger was doing.

Slowly and unsteadily he regained his feet and realised that he still held the bone between his teeth. With one hand he slowly removed it, then drawing his hand back he threw it across the midden where it landed in the pit in front of Roden. Her gaze did not move from him, her mouth now gaped open in a grin and she was panting. He could feel every hair on his body prickling in fear and he struggled to steady his breathing; taking a full lungful he screamed, 'Brak!', then after a few more deep breaths he screamed again, 'Brak!'.

In the long-house, Rat, who was feigning sleep, opened his eyes when he heard the calls but did not move; Brak, grunted and stirred but did not wake. Keeping very still, Sonty waited and listened for help coming, but there was only silence. He started to move back once more, slowly and carefully this time and eventually he felt the firm ground at the edge of the pit beneath his feet. He gathered his strength and his wind, then turning as fast as he could, he ran for his life. As he ran, he heard the rapid crunching of shells behind him as Roden crossed the pit in long bounds. The silence that followed, when Roden reached solid ground, was even more terrifying than the noise the shells had made. As he ran, he screamed,

'Brak, Brak!'

Brak heard the cries this time, rolled out of his bed and in the same action picked up his axe. Running for the door he bellowed,

'Rat, wake up, Sonty needs our help.'

Rat mumbled something and slowly sat up scratching his head.

'What, what is going on?'

'Move your arse, we need to go.'

Brak ran out of the door and around the corner of the long-house, where he stopped and peered to where he thought the shouts had come from.

As Sonty ran, too frightened to look back, he was taken by surprise to find that Roden was running effortlessly by his side. He looked down to find that she was looking up at him as they ran, stride for stride. Then in one move she overtook him and swerved across his path, her back was level with his waist so he somersaulted over her and crashed to the ground. Brak could not make out what was happening, so ran towards the blurred shapes in the distance, calling over his shoulder to Rat as he ran.

'Rat, Rat come help me.'

Sonty was winded and on his back when Roden came and stood over his body. He made himself as flat he could as if to escape into the ground, he could feel Roden's breath on his face and a drool of saliva fell from her jaws into his open mouth. He started to scream again,

'Bra...'

But the scream was choked off when Roden bent down, turned her head sideways to take his neck into her mouth, then closed her jaws. The shock of the pain jolted through his entire body, his hands came up and pushed futilely against her chest. Holding tightly, she shook him from side to side, his head bouncing backwards and forwards through a wide arc. Sonty was enveloped in blackness as his hands fell to his side. Even while she was killing him, Roden could hear the running feet of Brak and the roar of his war cry, her eyes tracked him as he came, but still she kept her hold until the last moment when Brak was almost upon them. She knew this old man and that he was not to be feared. With a deep throated growl and a last shake of his neck, she released her hold on Sonty, then she turned and trotted unhurriedly into the forest.

Brak saw the fuzzy dark shape separate into two, one laying on the ground and the other moving off into the forest, it was a wolf. He ran towards the prone figure of Sonty. As he came up to him he said,

'Speak to me boy, say something. Are you hurt? Make a noise, move, say something.'

As he finished speaking he was kneeling at Sonty's side. He put his hands around Sonty's neck and felt straightaway that it was broken, his shoulders sagged and he bent forwards until his head rested on Sonty's chest, devastated that his new found friend, a man from his own race who reminded him so much of his own son, was dead. Rat walked slowly towards them, watching Brak and wondering if he would be so grief-stricken if he, Rat, had perished. This boy had been here for just a little time, he could not understand why Brak was so desolate. He would surely have felt differently about the boy if he had known that Sonty would have killed and eaten them both. He knelt by Brak and put his hand on his shoulder, he could see by Sonty's twisted neck that he was dead.

'What has happened, is he alright?'

Brak still knelt by Sonty's side and did not move or raise his head from Sonty's chest. His voice was low, almost a whisper.

'Wolf, it was a wolf. That bitch-wolf has killed the boy. I do not understand why he was here alone, so far from the long-house.'

He let out a low groan.

'Well, he did say that he felt unwell, then he went

out and I fell asleep.'

Brak lifted his head from Sonty's chest, turned and thrust the palm of his hand onto Rat's neck, driving him back until he was bent over backwards, with his other hand he raised his axe behind his head. His face contorted in anger.

'You put something in that drink you gave him.' Then shouting in Rat's face, 'You are up to your shaman's tricks again. This is your handiwork you evil creature.'

Rat knew that despite their friendship, what he said next would decide whether he lived or if his head would be broken beneath Brak's axe. He thrust his hands out to stave off the fall of the axe but knew that they would not save him, Brak could kill him in one blow. He spoke urgently.

'Brak, stop, stop and think; you said yourself that the wolf killed Sonty, I was asleep in the long-house with you. Even as a shaman, I have no power over wolves. It is Roden you should hate, not me. I just assumed he had gone for a shit, he was holding his belly, perhaps the meal had upset his guts.'

Brak relaxed his hold on Rat's neck, lowered his axe and sat back. His arms slumped by his side and his head fell forwards. Rat sat by him and when he spoke his voice was filled with sorrow.

'This is dreadful, he was so young.'

Brak looked up and stared at Rat. He could not fathom his friend. Was he a good man or an evil one? Brak was bewildered by him: it was sad that he could know him as a friend for so much of his life, and yet he could not see what lay in his heart. He was shocked at his own response to Sonty's death, perhaps because Sonty was their new hope, young and full of life, and looking at his face now it was as if his only son lay dead before him. He decided to take action.

'The ground is too hard to bury him, we must give him a chief's farewell. Come let us start we have a long day ahead of us.'

Rat groaned inwardly, Brak intended to give Sonty his ending on a funeral pyre. It would take a lot of wood and they were both feeling weak from the lack of food. Brak stood, then bent down astride of Sonty's body; grasping his wrists he pulled him up then flipped the body onto his back, with Sonty's arms around his neck. Bent double, he set off for the long-house, Rat picked up Brak's axe and walked by his side. Looking across, he could see that Sonty's head, which lolled over Brak's shoulder, bounced up and down as Brak struggled along. He also saw that although he was now old, Brak's upper body was still so wide that the thin body of Sonty barely covered half the width of the old warrior. When Brak reached the long-house he carried the body inside and laid it gently down by an unused hearth. He turned to Rat.

'Come, come, we must hurry. Bring your knife and axe and we will set about building this pyre.'

All day they worked in silence, collecting bundles of wood and carrying them back to camp. Despite the cold, they were both sweating by the time that they had finished and they had a large pile of wood in the centre of the camp. Rat staggered into the long-house; not looking at the body of Sonty, he collapsed onto his bed and tried to sleep. Brak stomped after him into the long-house, walked up to Rat's bed and, seizing him by an ankle, pulled Rat from the bed to land with a bump face down on the floor.

'Light the pyre, you are better at it than me; hurry yourself, it is getting dark.'

With that, he released Rat's ankle, walked over to Sonty and once more pulled him onto his back. He carried him outside and laid him gently on top of the pile of wood. He straightened Sonty's legs and his clothes and folded his arms across his chest. He then climbed onto the pyre, straddling the body he whispered into the boy's ear.

'If I can revenge your death I will. Be at peace wherever you are. If you are with our ancestors, tell them that I will be coming soon to join you. It was good to know you boy.'

He placed a hand on either side of the boy's face and kissed him on the forehead.

'Go in peace Sonty.'

Then he jumped from the pyre and watched Rat as he set about starting the fire. It was fully dark by the time the fire took a hold sufficient for the heat to drive them back. Brak went to stand by his tusk; he wrapped one arm around it and stood motionless, his face glowing red from the flickering light. Rat went and sat in the doorway of the long-house with his chin in his cupped hands. He wondered if he and Brak were still friends and if they would find food tomorrow. He felt the heavy burden of being a shaman. He missed Suffi, if she were here he could talk to her about the ways of magic, she would understand how a shaman must work with the Earth Mother to achieve certain goals.

11

SUFFI

Rat had lived for sixteen summers when Suffi was born. A shaman always attended births; to give blessings to the newborn, or to offer death chants over the bodies of the mothers or their babies. So it was that on a gentle autumn night Sabal was summoned to attend a birth in the round-house of a young couple expecting their first baby to come into the world. On his way Sabal stopped to collect Rat.

'Come on Rat,' he shouted through the doorway of Rat's lodge. 'We have work to do for the Earth Mother and the tribe.'

Rat, who had been expecting the call, looked over to his father for permission to leave; his father turned away from staring into the fire for a moment to give Rat a cold look, then grunted his allowance, returning once more to stare into the flames. Rat used to wonder what his father saw in those embers, a man at war with himself and with the world, never happy for himself or for anyone else. Although Rat was very aware of how much his father resented his crippled presence, he also knew that this man had been cursed with sadness long before Rat had appeared to add to his burdens. He wished he could ease his misery, perhaps with some of Sabal's potions, but he would never dare to suggest this to his father. The thought to secretly slip such a potion into a drink to bring him some relief crossed his mind occasionally, but then his father would snarl at, or cuff Rat or his mother, and any thoughts of helping him died in the thinking.

Dressing hurriedly, he hobbled after Sabal and had caught up with him by the time they reached the doorway of the young couple's lodge. There were candles lit around the room, offering just enough light for the huddle of four old women surrounding the girl, Sosa, to see to their task. Sabal caught Rat's arm and pushed him against the wall, whispering in Rat's ear.

'Let the hags do their work. There will be time for us when they are done.'

Then he leaned against the wall, folded his arms and calmly watched the women at their work. This was the first birth that Rat had attended. He could see over the shoulders of the women that Sosa was squatting over a hay-lined hollow that had been scooped into the earth floor, with her head thrown back and her face a mask of pain that shocked and frightened Rat. She was holding onto the shoulders of two supporting women with a fierce grip. He caught the glance of her young man, Rufi, who was sat by the far wall, with an expression like a hare that had been caught in a snare, and gave him a smile of reassurance that he did not feel himself. The girl began to wail and cry out in pain, inwardly Rat winced but forced himself to carry on watching, for this was part of the Earth Mother's magic, to be revered as such. Drawn by the need to see this magic at work, Rat stepped away from the wall, shrugging off Sabal's catch on his elbow, to stand at the back of the woman crouching between the girl's knees.

This surely was magic, for a head started to appear between the girls legs, to be gently supported by the attending woman. Rat was biting on his bottom lip as he saw in the flickering light the body of the baby follow the head, then the arms appeared and lastly the legs, before the newborn baby dropped away from the girl to be cradled in the woman's hands. Still the women waited expectantly, then Rat saw the cord that still led from the baby and into the girl was dropping down, until a bloody piece of meat followed the baby and fell from the girl to be seized on by one of the women and the cord joining them was cut away. The baby was then gathered into the arms of the attending woman, while the girl collapsed to lie prostrate and covered in sweat on the earthen floor. Another woman took the bloody meat and set it to gently cook over the fire, to be fed to the mother when she was ready to eat. Rat was ecstatic to have witnessed this magic take place before his eyes, he glanced over his shoulder at Sabal who was looking very bored and impatient to finish his duties here.

Two of the women cleaned up the girl, then covered her in furs. The other two women were examining the baby from the top of its head to the end of its toes. Rat saw that they were shaking their heads and tutting to themselves. Sosa held out her arms and asked to hold her baby, but the women would not oblige and went over to Sabal who bent over the baby to see for himself where the women were pointing. He could be seen solemnly nodding in agreement with the women. The girl continued to ask for her baby, but instead Sabal went and knelt at her head and whispered in her ear. That was when she began to scream, she would not stop and was then held by two of the women to prevent her from getting to her feet. The noise was deafening, so Sabal took the baby from the women and jerked his head to Rat to leave the lodge with him at once. Once outside, Rat asked what was happening, but Sabal strode off at full pace and left Rat behind to hobble after him as fast as he could until they entered Sabal's empty dark round-house. Even so far away, they could still hear the now faint screams and entreaties of the girl. Placing the baby down uncovered and as far away from the fire as possible, Sabal lit two candles and sat by his hearth. Rat sat down on the other side to him and wondered what was wrong.

'Why have you taken that girl's baby? This cannot be right, you must give it back at once.'

Sabal nodded to where the baby lay in the dark.

'Go and look young Rat, I had no choice, she is

blind in one eye, she cannot be allowed to live, she would weaken the tribe.'

Rat went over to the baby and picked it up in his arms, then carried it back to the fire where the light was strongest. Gently pulling back the lids of her eyes, he could see that the left one was entirely white, Sabal was right, she was blind in that eye.

'But she is a girl, she could still forage and cook and do all the things that a woman would need to do. She could have a man and have children, she does not *need* this eye! Look at me,' he said, pointing to his deformed leg, 'do I make the tribe weaker, or will I make the tribe all the stronger when you have trained me to be a shaman? She must be given her chance also.'

'You were the last such baby to be allowed to live. You know that I and your father were for your death, but your mother fought so hard for your life, well you are here now. But the elders have decided. No baby that is not perfect is to live; I will take her to be left in the forest come the morning. Now return to your father's hearth and leave me in peace.'

Rat was devastated to hear that this baby was to die. Like him, she was not as she should be, but she could grow to be someone special, she just needed the chance to live and prove herself. Perhaps he could find a way.

'I will take her to the forest in the morning, if I am to be a shaman, I must do these things. Give me a chance to show my courage, let me do this for you. I will not let you down.'

He went over to where the baby lay naked in the darkness and gently covered her in a fur. He turned to Sabal, still sat gazing into the fire.

'Well, will you let me do this, will you wait for me come the morning?'

Sabal turned away from the fire and looked at him for a while, weighing him up.

'I will wait, be here early, just after the sun has risen, I will not wait any longer than that.'

Rat nodded his appreciation then left to return to his parent's round-house, where he lay and stared at the roof-beams the whole of the remaining night, too frightened to sleep and chance that he would be too late at Sabal's come the morning.

At the first sign of light, taking care not to wake his father, he rose and dressed, slipped his axe into his belt and left for Sabal's as the sun was just peeping above the ridge. When he entered the round-house he found it to be empty. Sabal had deceived him, guessing rightly that Rat had his own plans for the baby. He must find her before the wild beasts did but where to look? He hobbled around in circles wondering where to seek her. Sabal was lazy, he would not travel further than he must. As Sabal would have done, he checked the ridges for wolves and saw that the pack was resting high on the south ridge, so he headed for the edge of the forest below the north ridge. There was no sign of Sabal, he was far too crafty to return to camp directly from where he had left the baby. No, he would circle around and come back far away from where the small body must now be laying on the freezing cold ground.

There had been rain, so the ground was slippery beneath Rat's fumbling feet: he had to pull himself up by grabbing branches and pushing against tree trunks. When he had reached a height where the ground momentarily flattened off, he stopped and listened, nothing could be heard but the wind sighing high in the treetops. He fancied that Sabal would choose this flat area to leave her, but which way should he look, east or west? He chose east, towards where the sun was rising. He ran as fast as his leg would allow, then he would pause and listen, running again and again as he moved along the side of the valley. He leant against a tree trunk, sweat running down his forehead and into his eyes; as he raised an arm to wipe the sweat away he heard a faint cry.

Stumbling and running, he made his breathless way towards the crying. Coming to a clearing he saw the baby, naked of all clothing, on her back with her arms waving in the air as she cried out to continue living. Kneeling by her he lifted her and slipped her into his furs to warm next to his body. He stayed kneeling there, his skin prickling from the ice-coldness of her body. Putting his arms around the outside of his furs, he cuddled her into himself and wondered if what he had planned for her would work, and if she would live to the sunset of this day.

Once rested, he gathered his strength then set off to climb the ridge. It was now fully light but there was no heat in the sun, for which he was grateful, as he was sweating so much from the climb and the added burden of the baby. As she became bathed in his hot sweat, her body started to warm once more and he could feel her start to wriggle against him as he climbed up and up. When he came at last to stand on the ridge-top the cold wind soon began to chill him, so he wasted no time before descending down to the camp of the Grovi, wondering what sort of welcome his little companion would have there.

Arriving at the camp by mid-afternoon, he made his way to the long-house and came to sit by the hearth of Brak's family. The men and boys were away, so it was Brak's mother who welcomed him.

'Hello Rat, this is unexpected, what is that beneath your furs have you brought some game for me to cook?'

'Well, it is game of sorts but not for cooking.' He opened his furs to reveal the newborn baby lying against his chest. 'I need your help, or this little creature will die today.'

Brak's mother was shocked, instinctively she went

to pick the baby from his chest but then stopped herself. She spoke with anger in her voice.

'Have you stolen this baby? If you have then you have done a terrible thing Rat, not to be forgiven.'

Rat held up the palms of his hands in protest and shook his head from side to side.

'No, no, you must believe me. This poor thing is blind in one eye, so she was left in the forest to freeze to death or be consumed by beasts. My tribe would kill her, I have brought her to the Grovi to see if you will raise her. Will you save her for me?'

Brak's mother sat on her bed and thought, then she came over and took the baby from Rat. Holding her gently, she pulled back her eyelids and saw that indeed one eye was blind. She shook her head, not knowing what to say or do. When the other women saw that Brak's mother was holding a new baby, they left their hearths and gathered around, whispering and nudging one another.

'Do you see this sisters?' She held up the baby. 'Rat has brought us a baby, a baby who is blind in one eye, what shall we do with her eh?'

One of the women called out,

'Is this pup yours young Rat, we didn't think that you had it in you!'

Rat blushed and the women laughed. Brak's mother admonished them.

'While you laugh, this baby is going hungry, who has milk to spare for her? You Nolly, your young one is coming to leave your tits is he not, can you spare this one your milk?'

Nolly was a plump young woman who was always the first to help with the children and often had a trail of youngsters behind her when she was foraging. Good natured and motherly though she was, she was still unsure about taking a baby from a tribe of humans that were regarded as being bad people, ugly in their ways and ugly in their appearance. She pulled a face and held back, so Brak's mother stood and placed the baby into Nolly's arms. It had the desired effect, Nolly's face beamed down on the little one.

'I must first speak with my man, he will be more inclined to kill this thing than have to hunt and care for it.'

Brak's mother used her high status in the tribe to complete the deal.

'My man will speak with him, do not worry about that. He will accept this one and we will support you with food so that she will not go hungry. Will you take her, as a favour to me?'

As Nolly looked down on the baby cradled in her arms, it opened its eyes and cried out in hunger causing milk to dribble from Nolly's breasts, so she placed a nipple into its mouth and smiled as it started to hungrily feed. Brak's mother had her answer and Rat looked on with pride and enormous relief; he had achieved the first part of his plan.

He named the little girl Suffi and whenever he visited with the Grovi he would take food and trinkets for her. When she started to talk he would sit with her and talk to her only in the language of the Salar, so that as she grew she became, like himself, fluent in both languages. Early on he had sat with Nolly and explained that it was his intention to take Suffi back to live with the Salar when she was old enough. Nolly was not happy, but

Rat promised that he would bring Suffi back to visit with her so that she would not be entirely lost to her stepmother. Also, they would be able to spend their summers together on the hunting-plains, Nolly came to be content with that.

All that was in the future, for the time being, as she grew to be a girl, she was accepted by the Grovi as one of their own. She was bright and had a way with her that made people happier when they were with her. She fought to not be held back by her partial blindness, only the finest stitching would cause her problems. When defeated, she would burst into tears and throw the work onto the ground, but if left, she would return and try once more until she had stitched it to her satisfaction. She loved her stepmother, but Rat had insisted that Suffi always remembered that she was a member of the Salar tribe. She was not told that the Salar had tried to kill her though, instead she was told that her real mother had given her up to help bring the tribes together, and that one day she would meet her real mother and father again to live with the Salar as a full tribal member. Rat started her education, not just by teaching her the language of the Salar, but also the ways and history of her own tribe in readiness for her eventual return.

He implemented his final plan for Suffi when she was twelve summers old. He knew that when Sabal went to join the Earth Mother he would take over as the Shaman of the Salar; in order to maintain the unbroken line of knowledge of magic and medicine he would need to train someone to replace himself as Shaman when his own time came. If she was willing to take on such a difficult position, Suffi would be ideal. Rat had never been given a choice as to whether to become a shaman or not, there was no other role he could carry out in the tribe, but Suffi was different, she was performing very well as an active woman in her adopted tribe, she would have to be seduced into accepting his plan for her future.

He started gently, taking her for walks in the meadows and the forest, by the river and down to the sea. In each place, he would describe the creatures that lived there, how they survived, what they ate and how they served the Earth Mother. He would encourage her to accompany him when he was gathering herbs, special berries and other medicines and how they could make people well again. If one of the Grovi would fall ill, she would attend with him as his assistant, prepare and administer the medicines to them and then share in the thrill of seeing them get better once more. He explained to her that the Grovi had no gods, but that the Salar had the Earth Mother to look over them and keep them safe. She was not to talk of the Mother when she was alone with the Grovi, but she must instead keep her in her heart at all times and see everyday how the Mother worked her ways in the world. One day he showed her the small figure of the Earth Mother that he had secretly taken from Sabal's bag of magic possessions. Suffi took it from him and with her mouth open in awe turned it over in her hands.

'Is this her Uncle, the Earth Mother?'

'No little Suffi, this is not her, this is her symbol on earth, held by the Salar from beyond the beginning of time. She is very precious, Sabal would be furious with me if he found out that I had taken this to show you. It must never leave the tribe, but I wanted you to see it and understand. If you wish, I can show you how to be her servant on earth, but not until you return to the Salar. When Sabal has left this life behind, that will be when I can show you the secret things that only a shaman can know.'

Suffi nodded, he was slowly drawing her in. Although the Grovi thought her rather plain, by Salar standards she was growing into a beautiful young woman, with strong features and long black hair that she grew to fall over her left eye. Covered most of the time as it was, it was even more of a shock when her hair would fall away to expose the dull white of her blind eye. The time finally came when Sabal departed to join the Earth Mother. In the week of his dying Rat tried every potion and chant that he could think of to save him, but Sabal continued wasting away until he was little more than a skeleton beneath the bedding. One day when Rat tried to make him drink his latest attempt at a healing potion, Sabal put up a bony hand to his chest to stop him. His voice was little more than a whisper, so low that Rat had to place his ear to his mouth to understand what he was saying.

'No more, no more, I am ready to go to her Rat, leave me be, let me sleep my way to her.'

Rat stood back then looked down on him; he had no affection for the old man but he had been taught well by him, and he felt more than ready to take over as Shaman to look after the spiritual and medical needs of the tribe. He turned his back on Sabal and left him in the dark round-house to die alone.

The tribe had never been fond of Sabal, but he had never felt the need for people to love him, his duty had a higher calling. Despite their indifference at his passing they saw him off with all due ceremony. Then it was time for Rat to take his place as the Shaman of the Salar, a role he had waited patiently for his whole life. This was a significant time for them all, a shaman carried the soul of the tribe, so merited a sacrifice. There was feasting for three days, and on the last night of the last day Rat was called to stand before Dalkan the Chief and the elders before a great fire. The young women of the tribe who had not yet selected a man for themselves stood around him and stripped him naked, then dressed him in his ceremonial robes; the Chief stepped forwards at the last to place the mask over Rat's head. As the mask slipped over his head he felt transformed in that moment to be a true shaman, capable of great magic, he was fulfilled at last.

He turned away from the fire, and through the eyeholes in his mask saw his first sacrificial offering kneeling before him; a young man found wandering in the valley had been taken prisoner as Sabal had started his journey to death. He had been held in readiness for this ceremony and Rat would pass him, guarded by two hunters, on his way to visit the dying shaman. The boy was young and frightened but he was no fool, his own tribe sacrificed young men. He tried desperately to befriend his guards, perhaps if they grew to like him they would spare his life. It was to no avail, so this night found him kneeling, hands tied behind him, with his back to Rat. If he could have seen the black apparition that stood behind him he would have fainted with fear. Rat took the braided leather necklace and stepped forwards to drop it over the boy's neck, he could see that he was shaking so much that his whole body seemed to vibrate. Quickly slipping the short stick through the necklace, he twisted it as fast as he could, struggling to brace himself as the boy began to jerk away from his tormentor. Eventually the boy became still and slipped to the ground, Rat followed him down and maintained the pressure until he was sure that he was dead, then he relaxed his hold on him and stepped back, turning to the surrounding tribe he lifted his arms high to receive the loud calls and cheers. He watched as the body was taken away to be dropped into the marsh, and swore in that moment that future sacrifices would never know their fate in advance. They would die drugged, they would go to the Earth Mother happy. Many years later, he would keep that promise to himself when he sacrificed young Polus.

Once he became established as the tribe's shaman, his standing in the tribe grew until he stood only behind the Chief in power. He made a point of allying himself closely with his chief and the elders; Sabal had always been an aloof character but this was not the type of shaman that Rat chose to be. The closer to Dalkan he was and the more enmeshed into the fabric of the tribe he could become, the more he could do to bring about his plan to make the two tribes allies and to bring Suffi back home to live with the Salar as his assistant. He was patient and bided his time, a year went by before an opportunity presented itself when one of Dalkan's children fell ill with a fever.

Only four summers old, the little one was close to death within days of failing to rise from his bed one morning. He was bathed in sweat and could not be woken, his mother was distraught with grief. Rat took Dalkan to one side and warned him that his condition was very serious and that prayers should be made to the Earth Mother for his recovery. He dressed in his robes and mask, then gathered the family around the bed of the boy and led them in chants and prayers. When he was satisfied that all that could be done spiritually had been attended to, he removed his mask then took a powerful potion from his bag, this drink would either kill the child or save him, then he went to lay on the bed alongside the boy. Pulling apart his jaws, he poured the liquid slowly into his mouth while massaging his throat to ensure that it was swallowed. Then he lay down beside him and held him close to await the outcome. He slept alongside the boy while his mother and his aunts sat around the bed and sang and prayed.

In the early dawn light he looked at the boy and saw that his eyes were open and looking at Rat, wondering why the tribe's shaman was lying next to him on the bed. The fever had passed and he was back to his normal self, as if nothing had befallen him. Suddenly he jumped out of the bed and threw himself into his mother's bed, where she joined him and snuggled down with him. His parents were overjoyed to see their little boy restored to life, and Dalkan came over to the still prone Rat and hugged him in gratitude. Still Rat waited for his moment, and it came when one day he and Dalkan were sat alone by Rat's hearth, the mood was convivial, the men felt almost like brothers, they were so close. Rat knew that now the time had come to speak out.

'You are my Chief, Dalkan, I respect and love you for that but I must confess I did something that was against yours and Sabal's wishes. I do not regret this thing but I would have you know it and decide how you will deal with me.'

Dalkan looked at him sharply and placed his hands on his knees, his relaxed mood was gone.

'You have my interest Rat, tell me, what have you

done?'

Rat had rehearsed this conversation many times in his head, but now that he was sat opposite the now fierce looking Dalkan he struggled to find the words.

'Fifteen summers ago, a baby was born to Rufi and Sosa.'

'Yes I remember, she was blind in one eye. Sabal told me that he did the right thing and left her in the forest to die. They have had healthy babies since, why are you still concerned?'

'The baby, well the baby, she did not die, she is alive and living with the Grovi.'

Dalkan looked as if he had been slapped in the face, Rat could not gauge yet how angry he was, he looked so shocked. It was only in the telling of the tale that Rat realised the import of what he had done: breaking the law of the elders and then taking the child to live with a tribe of different humans that, while not enemies to go to war with, were a constant source of friction while competing for game and food.

'Rufi and Sosa, do they know what you did with the child, did they ask that you do this?'

'No, no, it was just me, look at this leg of mine, with your laws I would not be sat opposite you now and your child who I saved would be dead. Those who are born different should at least be allowed to *try* and live, if they fail then that is the Earth Mother's will, let her decide.'

'Why do you tell me this now? Before I discuss your crime with the elders, what is it that you want? You must want something from me, or you would never have confessed to this crime.'

'With your blessing, I desire two things, the first is that I wish to bring this girl, she is called Suffi, back to the tribe; she is a Salar woman, she should be here with us. You should know that I have been training her to be a shaman, she is good, and when I pass she should be the one to replace me. This tribe needs her.'

'Second, I wish for the two tribes to become allies and work together, not to hate or be suspicious of each other. I have lived with them, they are not so different from us and we can learn much from them on the summer-hunting-plains.'

Then, praying that he was not going too far with his chief,

'You will not like this but their hunters are better than ours.'

Dalkan glared at him, Rat gulped, he *had* gone too far. Dalkan stood, still staring at him, his face expressionless.

'I will discuss this with the elders, then you will be called to hear your fate.'

Then he turned and walked out of Rat's round-house. Rat stared into the fire and wondered if his years of study to become the tribe's shaman, and all of his planning and scheming would come to nothing. He sat motionless by his hearth all of that day and into the night, when an elder appeared at the doorway and summoned him to attend the Chief. With a sigh, Rat stood and made his way, feeling very alone, to the large round-house where his Chief held court. He entered and went to stand before the Chief and the elders, nodded to each in turn then waited to hear their decision. Dalkan looked around the crowded lodge, most of the tribe had heard of the scandal and were waiting to see how their Chief would deal with this law-breaker.

'Rat, I have taken counsel from the elders of the tribe. You were wrong to take the child, the tribal law says that she should rightly have died. However, she lives, she has grown to be a woman and, from what you have told me, she has a role here with the Salar. You have our permission to bring her back to her mother and father. You have asked if we can form bonds with the beasts that live in the next valley, of this we are not so sure. They are not civilised like the Salar.'

With difficulty, Rat let this pass.

'They do not respect our boundaries for hunting and foraging.'

Again, Rat wanted to blurt out that because the tribes did not talk to each other there were no agreed boundaries, but he kept his silence.

'You also say that their hunters are better than our hunters.'

There was angry murmuring from the watching

crowd.

'We doubt that. Have you anything to say for yourself?'

'Great Chief, I only ask that I be given permission to arrange a meeting between some of their elders and ours; they could meet on the ridge between our two valleys, I would attend and translate for both tribes. I ask no more than that, one meeting, if then our elders say no more that will be an end of it.'

Dalkan leaned over to speak with the elders at his side, some were shaking their heads and some were nodding, Rat could only guess what they would decide. Then Dalkan addressed Rat once more.

'We have decided to allow this one meeting only, if that goes well there will be others, if not, well we have lost nothing by it. Arrange it soon.'

Rat was very relieved, he had achieved all he could have hoped for. Dalkan beckoned him to come close, then the Chief stretched out his hand and took Rat by the back of his neck and pulled him close enough to whisper in his ear.

'You have got what you wanted little Rat but hear

this, break any laws in future or cross me again, and I will see to it that you are punished, severely punished, do you hear me?'

Rat nodded vigorously, then Dalkan released his hold on his neck and allowed Rat to stand upright once more. Stepping back, Rat spoke to his Chief.

'Great Chief, I thank you for your forgiveness and clemency, I will never let you down again.'

With that, he turned clumsily and, with as much dignity as he could muster, hobbled out of the lodge into the dark night and straight into the fat arms of Sosa. Rat could see Rufi beaming at him over Sosa's shoulder,

'Sosa and I thank you for taking our baby, you saved her life and now you are going to bring her back to us.' He stepped forward and leaned over his woman to place a hand on Rat's shoulder. 'As you know, we have other children, but to have our first-born again, well, we look forward to see the woman that she has become.'

Rat was still locked in Sosa's embrace, she had put on weight over the years and was almost overpowering him. He raised his hands to push her arms away to let him breathe again. Eventually Sosa stepped back, her face wet with tears. Rat tried to prepare them to meet with their long lost daughter.

'I did it for the child, like me she is not perfect, but she deserved a life and now she has one. In a few days I will go to the Grovi and bring her back to you and the tribe. You will need to be patient with her, she has grown up with that tribe and their ways. She might seem strange to you at first but, given time, she will become a Salar woman again I promise you.'

Rat had always told Suffi that one day she would have to leave the Grovi and the family that had brought her up, but when he sat in the long-house and told her that she would be leaving that day she was distraught. She threw her arms around her stepmother Nolly and would not let go. For her part, Nolly was also inconsolable; when she was finally separated from Suffi she threw herself onto her bed and wept. Rat tried to ease their sorrow.

'I will bring Suffi back to you, she is not gone

forever and she will do well with the Salar under my protection. Let her go, for her sake, let there be tears today and there will be smiles in future days I promise you. Come, you must both be brave, say your farewells, for today at least.'

And so it was that Suffi turned her face away from her adopted family and tribe to follow Rat and live with strangers in a foreign valley. She did this for Rat, he owned her life, she owed everything to this man she called 'Uncle' and she trusted him. When they arrived at the Salar's camp, Rufi and Sosa who had once lost a baby, were, thanks to Rat, given back a strikingly beautiful young woman, with long black hair and high cheekbones that gave her a look that demanded respect. She even smelt differently from them and had an air of mystery about her that they found a little intimidating. After the initial hugs, tears and laughter, Sosa and Rufi made her welcome in their peculiar little round-house and slowly Suffi began to learn the ways of this new tribe.

Over the following years, Rat showed her how to become a powerful shaman and she grew to be a valued tribal member. Valued though she was, no man would take her for his woman, they were happy to sleep with her, but being blind in one eye she was not whole and, even worse, she practised magic with the tribe's Shaman. No man was prepared to risk that she might secretly use her magic powers on him. Rat did not, despite his promise, ever take her back to visit the Grovi, but when the time of the shared summer-hunting took place on the plains, she would go and live for those golden months in great happiness with her stepmother Nolly and all of her adopted family.

12

SICKNESS

That night Rat cooked the remaining crayfish but Brak, who had taken to his bed as soon as the pyre had burnt out, was not interested in food. He had turned his back to Rat and would not answer Rat's entreaties.

'Come on Brak, you must eat something. I know that you are upset at Sonty's passing but you not eating will not bring him back to us. I am sure that he would have wanted you to survive the winter, come on man eat.'

Rat was sure that Brak was not sleeping and seemed so desolate in his silence. Rat sat and ate his portion, watching his friend's naked back in the firelight. There were scars across his still muscled back from his life of hunting and fighting. When Rat was finished eating he placed Brak's bowl down at the cold end of the long-house, hoping that his friend would find his hunger again soon. Sleep came eventually and when he woke in the morning he looked first to check on Brak, but he had not moved in his bed. Rat went over to him and placed his hand gently on Brak's shoulder.

'Brak my friend, speak to me. I am worried, are you sickening for something, are you unwell?'

But Brak still did not move, not even to shrug Rat's hand away. Rat could feel the warmth of his shoulder so he knew that he was alive. He pulled the furs up across Brak's back and shoulders to keep him warm.

'Will you drink some water, mmm? Please speak to me, I am your friend Rat, speak to me Brak so I need not worry.'

Brak still did not speak or move in response, so, exasperated, Rat turned and walked outside. It was a bright morning, the light making him squint his eyes as it reflected from the snow. He walked over to the remains of the pyre and found Sonty's skull and some bones, charred black among the ashes. He crouched down next to where the skull lay gazing up at the sky.

'You left me with no choice Sonty. You were going to kill Brak and I when the food ran out, I could not wait for that time, feigning sleep with one eye open, in case you came for me while you thought I was asleep. But I liked you boy, despite what you had done and were going to do. I do not think that you were evil, you were just trying to survive were you not? It was either you who was going to survive, or Brak and I, so here you are now, bones and ashes.'

He knelt and prayed for Sonty, asking the Earth Mother to take him and see that he did not go hungry again. He prayed for Brak, so that he would recover to become himself again and once more be his friend. Lastly, he prayed for himself, that he would live through the winter and find a way to keep Brak alive, so that they both might see spring come back to the valleys. Grunting like the old man he was, he stood once more and looked around the camp. There was nothing to keep them here, they must leave and go to his own valley where there might be something for them to eat. Also, Rat's small round-house would be much easier to keep warm when the full winter storms hit the valleys. But first he must make Brak well again.

He returned to the long-house and sat on his bed; with his head in his hands he watched Brak's unmoving back. He must do something to change this, so he took rocks from the fire to heat water and looked in his herb bag for what he needed, something that would put warmth back in Brak's soul. He went to the end of the long-house, took the bowl of cooked crayfish and returned to the hearth where he shelled the crayfish and shredded the meat, finally adding it with the herbs to the now hot water. He sat on the edge of Brak's bed, putting the bowl on the floor, he put his hands on Brak's shoulders and twisted him around to face him. Brak opened his eyes and Rat saw that they were dull and lifeless, still he would not speak. Rat switched position so that he could sit by Brak's head, then he raised the grizzled head and placed it on his lap.

Reaching down, he grasped the bowl from the floor and pushed it between Brak's closed dry lips. Tipping the bowl, some liquid spilled out and ran down Brak's cheeks onto the bedding. The drink was too precious to waste, so Rat slipped his fingers into Brak's mouth, found a gap between his teeth and prised his jaws apart, then slowly poured the liquid into his mouth. Brak gagged, then swallowed a mouthful. Rat poured more and Brak swallowed, and so it was until Brak had drunk all of the bowl's contents. Then he gently lifted Brak's head from his lap and lowered it back onto the bed. Standing, he looked down at his friend who had once more closed his eyes and turned away from him.

He started preparing for the trek back to the Salar's old camp. He rolled up his bedding and filled sacks with all the things they would need. He then went outside with their axes and spears, finding a suitable rock, he spent a long time grinding fresh edges on the weapons. He took the wolf-spear from where it was propped up against the wall of the long-house and checked the points at each end, they were still sharp. Taking some bladders, he went down to the river and filled enough to drink on the journey. When he was satisfied that he had done all that he could, he sat back on his bed and thought about what could be done with Brak. He smiled as a possible solution came to him.

'Brak, I know that you are not asleep. I have something to tell you, I need to tell you this, are you listening eh?'

Brak did not move or speak.

'Well, after my Asa died, I came to your camp to visit with you but you had gone hunting with all of the men. The women were out foraging and only Culu was left behind with the children to look after. I found her alone in this long-house with the babies. That was some woman, that Culu of yours, I had always found her attractive, she just had that look that would make your heart beat faster, eh Brak? I was lonely without a woman and just being near Culu made me hard.'

He stopped talking. Brak rolled onto his back with his eyes closed but still did not speak. Rat remained silent for a while. Then he spoke again.

'I was sat here on this bed talking to her while she prepared some food for me by your hearth, it got too much for me Brak, I had to have her. As she came to give me the bowl of food I stood up, took out my hard member and leaned in to kiss her.'

Again he fell silent. Brak opened his eyes and turned his head to look at Rat. After a pause he finally spoke in an angry demanding voice.

'What happened?'

Sounding slightly indignant, Rat replied.

'She tipped the bowl of food over my head and then punched me in the face. She knocked me over this bed onto my back. Then when I was on all fours trying to get away, she kicked me up the arse, she kicked me all the way out of the long-house. I had to wait outside until you and the other men came back.'

Rat could see that Brak was smiling, then he heard him softly chuckling.

'Oh yes, she was some woman my Culu, you were lucky to escape with your balls Rat.'

Rat was relieved to see Brak happy at the memory of Culu, but he was not the Brak he had been yesterday morning. It seemed as if the death of the boy had broken something inside of him, and that the dead Sonty was going to kill Brak as surely as the living one would have done. He had wanted to leave the camp today, but Brak was not ready yet, it would have to be tomorrow.

'Brak, I need your help. We must go to my old camp. I know my valley better than this one, I may be able to find us some food there and my round-house will keep us warmer when the winter storms come. We need to leave tomorrow, today we must find some meat and I think I know how we can find some.'

Brak turned on his side and looked quizzically at Rat.

'Meat, you say, there is no meat to be had. I am a hunter, I should know.'

'You may be a hunter but no one understands the ways of the creatures better than I do. When we were in the river yesterday I saw a slight chance for us. Come on Brak, rouse yourself, let us go and get some meat for you.'

Rat reminded Brak of the first creatures that the children of both tribes would hunt for first, ground squirrels. Very few were ever caught, as they had lookouts and disappeared into their burrows at the slightest alarm.

'But,' said Rat, 'in the winter they stay out of sight and sleep in their burrows until the spring comes again to warm the land. The ground is too hard to dig them out now, but when we were in the river I noticed that one high bank on a bend was by the edge of their burrows. If we take our axes to that bank, we may be able to catch them while they sleep. What do you say, shall we try?'

Brak sat and scratched at his beard while he thought. They had no food and these were desperate times for them both.

'Come then Rat, we will try, although I have my doubts that this will work. We will take the axes and some sacks, but bring the wolf-spear as well in case we meet Roden and her family out there.'

As they left the long-house, Rat kept Brak far enough away from the ashes of the pyre so that his blurred sight would not see Sonty's skull. Once more they made their way to the river, this time they were two and not three. For reasons neither could understand, without Sonty the landscape now felt empty and threatening to the two old men. Rat was having to keep watch for them both; he led with Brak's hand on his shoulder, looking from side to side and back the way that they had come, all the way to the river. He guided them to the place where on the far side of the river a high bank of sandy soil could be seen, a warm orange colour against the white of the snow and the black of the river. Rat dropped the wolf-spear on the river bank and they entered the freezing cold knee-high water, the mood was sombre and there was no singing this morning.

When they reached the far bank, Rat took Brak's hand from his shoulder and positioned him to one side. Together they started to attack the bank with their axes, the soil breaking away easily and falling into the river with loud splashes. Brak tired quickly and had to take many breaks to regain his breath. Rat encouraged him to keep going.

'Come on warrior, we must keep at it or we will not eat tonight.'

Then Rat saw that one of Brak's blows had exposed a bundle of dry grass.

'Stop Brak, stop.'

He stood in front of Brak and slowly and gently pushed his hands into the grass. Almost straightaway he felt the curled body of a squirrel, cold and still. He withdrew the creature in its ball of grass and laid it with care into his bag. He slapped Brak on the shoulder.

'You did it, what a hunter you are eh? We can save ourselves for now Brak and we will eat meat tonight. Come on, keep striking until our bags are full.'

They followed the tracks of the burrows from chamber to chamber, and in almost all they found one, sometimes two, squirrels sleeping there. Their bags were full by the time the sun had moved across the sky to lie low on the horizon. They put away their axes and Brak placed his hand once more on Rat's shoulder. Crossing back across the river they climbed the bank, Rat bending down in one movement to pick up the wolf-spear as they passed. Looking all around he could see no sign of life, he did not see that high above them two crows circled slowly across the grey sky. The men's legs and feet were so cold and numb that they seemed to be walking without touching the ground beneath them. Retracing their earlier footsteps in the snow, they made their way wearily back to camp.

Rat propped the wolf-spear up by the door and then hung the bags in the high beams at the cold end of the long-house, just beneath the layer of snow on the roof. He wanted these creatures to sleep on until he was ready to use them. With Brak's arm still on his shoulder he made his way to their beds, where they both sat and warmed their legs by the fire until some feeling returned painfully once more to their frozen limbs. Then Brak fell back on his bed and pulled the furs about his body. He fell asleep at once. Rat built up the fire, then lay back on his bed looking at Brak. He was sure that his friend was giving up on life and preparing to die; he had seen this with the old of both tribes many times before. If Rat were not here Brak would not have left his bed again, he had only agreed to go to the river to find food for Rat's sake.

Night fell rapidly and the long-house was everywhere dark, except for the glow around the hearth. Although no hunter, Rat was an expert at butchery, so he made short work of killing and preparing both sacks full of squirrels. He set them to roast over the fire on slender wet branches of willow. While Rat was moving around the long-house preparing the meal, his shadow cast grotesque shapes that swept back and forth across the walls and floor, and as he sat in front of the hearth to tend the fire, his now still shadow covered the sleeping Brak in darkness. When the meat was cooked he hung one sack of squirrels back on the roof beam, then he tried to rouse Brak to feed him, but he would not waken. He was lost in dreams of his now dead woman, Culu.

13

CULU

Early one morning during a blazing hot summer, Culu was born into the Grovi tribe on the hunting-plains. Her family had high status in the tribe, her father, Varsi, being one of the closest friends of the Chief and a fine hunter. Her mother, Mossy, was known in the tribe for her striking good looks and a fierce temper. She had lived for fifteen summers when Culu came, the first child for her mother, to be followed in the years to come by two sisters and a brother. For all his reputation as a hunter and warrior, her father was a kind man, who smilingly fended off the slaps and blows dished out by Mossy when she was in a rage. He loved his children, and each in turn as they grew older would spend time sat on his shoulders, watching the hunting from a distance, sometimes to be gently lifted and placed on the ground when, concerned for the safety of his men, he would run off to assist them with the hunt.

As she grew older, Culu would spend more time playing with the boys than she would with the girls and could outrun and outfight many of them. Because the boys would not let her join in when they practised using spears, axes and knives, she would go off somewhere on her own and train herself until she too was expert in their use. In particular, she trained herself to use the hunting spear, thinner than a normal spear, it was flighted with feathers for accuracy; when used with a throwing stick it had deadly power and range, more than enough power to penetrate the toughest of hides. When she was satisfied that she could wield her weapons as well as any man, she took to carrying them with her wherever she went, much to Mossy's displeasure.

Like all of the Grovi, she was at home in the river and the sea, and when she was not on the plains she would often be found swimming and diving around the rocky shore or splashing and playing in the river. What she did not like to do was to go foraging with the women, she would soon become bored and restless. Mossy would rebuke her and tell her that this is what the women of the tribe did, the men would hunt and the women would forage for food. Reluctantly, she would do as her mother said, but sulked and would not join in with the gossipy chat, instead finding ways to move further away from the group of women and forage for herself.

One day when she was thirteen summers old, the women were foraging far from the camp where the forest trees thinned before the ground climbed up to the high ridge. After collecting mushrooms and berries and almost filling their baskets, they sat down in a clearing to rest and to eat. Culu, working alone further up the slope gave them a resentful glance and continued to forage. The women were passing each other food, chewing on titbits and talking about the men, often giggling with each other with hands over their mouths. Two young men, strangers to the tribe, entered the clearing and came and sat in among the group of women. Mossy and the other matriarchs were wary, these men were armed with axes, and in any case, men should not approach women they did not know without permission. Some of the girls were interested in the young men, one in particular was rather handsome. The men looked about at the women, smiling at the young ones and nodding to the older women. The handsome one spoke,

'Will you pretty women share your food with us? We have not eaten for days and our bellies are rumbling.'

Mossy spoke up, in a voice that was neither friendly nor hostile,

'We can give you some food, but perhaps you could take what we offer and go on your way, we have more work to do before we return to camp.'

Smiling while he spoke the handsome one said,

'I think that you must be far from your camp old woman and with no men to guard you. That is not good, there are dangerous men in these forests, perhaps we should stay and protect you?'

The young girls giggled when they heard his words, they might like these men to stay a while longer. Mossy and the other older women exchanged glances, she did not like what he intended in his words. Her temper started to rise; she stood up and taking an empty basket she briskly filled it with berries and mushrooms from the others. She took it and stood in front of the men, holding out the basket she sternly said,

'Here, take this and be on your way, we are done here.'

Neither man took the basket and remained sitting where they were. They whispered to each other then suddenly stood, causing Mossy to take a step back still holding the basket. The handsome one scratched his face as if deep in thought, then spoke,

'We will go then, but I fancy we will take one of your young girls with us.'

He strode rapidly up to where the girls were sat together, took one by the wrist and pulled her up in one continuous movement, sweeping her off her feet and over his back. With his free hand he took out his axe. While Mossy was staring at what was happening, his companion snatched the basket of food from her hands, transferred it to under one arm then took out his own axe. The captured girl was struggling and screaming for help as the men began to back away into the forest. The handsome one bowed to Mossy with the girl still draped over his shoulders.

'You have been most generous old woman, we thank you and go. I hope that we meet again.'

They turned together to walk off into the forest and saw that directly ahead of them was a young girl. Culu was holding a hunting spear in her left hand, and in the other a throwing stick that was notched onto the back of the spear. Nobody moved, the men looked at the girl and she looked steadfastly back at them, suddenly her arms came back and in one swift movement the spear was hurled forward, flying across the short space to bury itself into the chest of the handsome man. The girl on his back could feel the tip of the spear pricking her side before he dropped her, then he fell backwards to lay over her, the spear shaft pointing straight up at the sky.

His companion's mouth fell open, he was frozen in shock at what had just happened. He was still holding the basket of food when the rock that Mossy was swinging with all of her force at the back of his head made contact. He dropped the basket and his axe and fell to his knees. Blacking out for a moment, when he came to he looked to see the young girl was now standing in front of him, with an axe held in her two small hands that was being drawn fully back. He watched it pause there behind her head, he smiled at her, she smiled back, then she brought the axe down in an arc to crush his skull.

Few men in the tribe had killed a man, so for a girl of thirteen summers to kill two men in one encounter was remarkable. A celebratory feast was held in her honour and her father was filled with pride at the reflected glory of her bravery. For the young men of the tribe it created a difficulty, it would not be seemly if your woman was a more fierce warrior than you. She was the most attractive of the young women, but none of the men would feel they were master in such a relationship. So it was that, while all the young men admired and wanted her, no one would step forward to claim her from her family. Brak was once such young man, two summers older than Culu, he also wanted her but, given the notorious temper that she had inherited from her mother, he knew he would never be able control her when he had not killed a man or performed some other great deed. He waited and watched her, and hoped that some other man would not take her before he had earned the right to ask.

Fortunately for Brak, his status in the tribe was changed forever after he had killed the sea monster. Previously, he had shown himself to be a good hunter and fighter, but his battle in the sea was the making of him and he was now regarded as a great warrior. He swore to himself that when the tribe went to the summer-hunting, he would ask her family if he would be allowed to take her to be his woman, and so it was. Their early years together were turbulent, as they both had quick tempers and were used to getting their own way. It was a shock for both to find that they were now bound to someone who was equally volatile. Neither would back down from the other during arguments, so Brak would often storm off to go hunting with the men.

When he would return some days later, their tempers were usually sufficiently cooled for a making up with each other. These reconciliations during the night in the long-house were so noisy that mothers would cover their children's ears, and everyone else pulled bedding over their heads to deaden the sounds that went on for most of the night. No one got much sleep on those nights, but the next day would find Brak and Culu much calmer and loving with each other. Children would be a consequence of these reconciliations, the first, Trovi, was a boy, to be followed by three sisters.

Brak was twenty two summers old when the old Chief died. Although there were older, more experienced hunters in the tribe, most thought Brak was the right man to replace him. His temper had eased slightly now and he had the charisma to bind the tribe together, supported as he was by his powerful woman. Becoming a chief changed Brak, the responsibility made him into a man who thought before he acted, who had to consider others and how they would react to his demands. He also had to be strong enough to discipline any man or woman who broke the rules of the tribe. They could be punished in many ways, being excluded from the tribe for a short time, or if the crime was severe, to be permanently exiled. Beatings would be given when necessary, but it was rare to directly kill a fellow tribal member, it was enough to exile them, which in itself was usually a death sentence. Brak and Culu had a good life together, they were leaders of their tribe, food was plentiful, the summers were hot and their children grew up healthy and strong.

They were old when their lives changed dramatically for the worse. The mammoths were few now and had no young to follow them across the plains. The weather changed, the summers were wet and the winters too long. The food stocks began to dwindle, and with so many mouths to feed Brak was in despair as to how he could feed his tribe. After three severe winters and a summer blighted by continuous rain, they were starving and dying. The old died first and then the children. One day during the last winter, when they found that they were alone in the long-house, Brak looked at Culu and, despite his now poor eyesight, he could see that Culu had become terribly thin. When he lay holding her in bed at night there was little substance to her, he could feel all of her ribs under his hands. He suspected that she was making sure that he and the grandchildren were getting enough food by going hungry herself. He sat by her on the bed and took her by the hand.

'Dear woman, when this winter is over and after the tribe have been to the plains, we must go south to the old lands. This valley has nothing left to give us.

We will prosper where the sun shines again. Let that thought keep you going during this cold winter.' He put out a hand and lifted her chin to look at him. 'Shall we go then?'

Culu smiled at him, her face was thin and there were wrinkles around her eyes, but she was still his beautiful Culu. She saw the deep lines in his face and that his hair and beard was grey, but still he looked like the chief that he was. She removed his hand and moved to sit next to him and laid her head on his chest.

'Brak, listen to me, the tribe must go but we will not be going with them. Do not be foolish, we are too old to travel so far and you cannot see well enough. Our time is done, so we will remain behind in this valley, together. When our tribe enters the old valleys, there will be tribes already living there, there will be fighting and conflict, only the young and strong must go, not us Brak, not us.'

She did not say it, but in her heart she knew that, like the two of her grandchildren who had died this winter, she would not live long enough to see the snow melt. She was happy, she had lived a good life with a good man, she had children and grandchildren, it was enough for her. From that day she slowly diminished and grew weaker. Her only sadness was the loss of their son Trovi to the Salar, but at least she knew that he was alive. Still, everyday she smiled and was happy, especially when the remaining grandchildren came and stood around her bed. She would take the babies into bed with her and sleep with them. They kept her warm and she loved the milky smell of their breaths on her cheek. Her daughters insisted that she must eat something, but she said that she was not hungry and that the food should be given to the children. If they insisted she would turn away and face the wall until, shaking their heads, they would leave her bedside. Brak felt helpless in the face of his wife's implacable path to death. He would hold her at night and with an ear to her mouth would listen to her feathery breathing, if she stopped breathing for a moment he would hold his own breath until she breathed again.

When he woke one morning, Culu had one hand draped around his neck and her face was pressed against his chest. For a moment he did not move, not wanting to disturb her, then he realised that the hand on his neck was cold. He raised his arm and placed his hand around her neck, there was no beat of life. He felt his world drop away from him, he was falling into a bottomless pit of misery, what would he do without his woman? He lay there, not moving, perhaps if he kept still she might yet wake, open her eyes and smile at him. A tear grew in the corner of his eye and fell onto Culu's cheek. He could hear his family and other members of the tribe waking and moving about the long-house, banging pots and stoking fires. There was laughter and chatter, a baby started to cry.

Outside, in a clear blue sky the sun shone brightly down on the camp. An icicle hanging from the eaves of the long-house shimmered in the light, slowly a drop of water grew in size before running down the length of the icicle, pausing at the tip, it released itself to fall onto the brilliant white snow below. Spring had arrived in the valley.

14

THE TESTING OF BRAK

Brak had been the Chief of the Grovi for ten summers when he almost lost his tribe, his valley and his life. It was a warm sunny morning when a small group of men entered the valley. They were first seen by a foraging party and not long afterwards a young girl came running, breathless, into the camp. Standing before Brak with sweat running down her face and her chest heaving from the strain, she spluttered out her message.

'There are men coming into our valley, strange men, not the Salar but men like them.'

'Have they attacked the women with you, are any hurt?'

She shook her head from side to side, paused to regain her breath, then,

'No, they are friendly, they have a boy with them who speaks as we do, he asked for me to run ahead and warn you that they are coming, also that they are peaceful and wish no harm, they just want to be allowed into the camp without being attacked.'

Brak put his hands on her shoulders to calm her.

'Go back and tell them that they are welcome to enter the camp, if they come to us in peace.'

The girl nodded and, still slightly out of breath, made her way back out of the camp to find the men.

Brak made use of the time to prepare for the visitors. The women who were not out foraging were told to stay with the children in the long-house, then he stood by his tusk in the centre of the camp, surrounded by his now heavily armed men. They waited there until late afternoon, when five men and a boy appeared from out of the forest. Dropping their many weapons at the edge of the camp, they made their way over to Brak and his men. The strangers held their hands open with their palms facing outwards, to show that they were not carrying weapons and that their intentions were peaceful, all except for the man who was the obvious leader of the group. He had his left hand on the back of the neck of a boy who looked like he was from a tribe like the Grovi, rather than his Salar-looking companions. The strangers were smiling all about them, in particular their leader was radiating friendliness, especially directed at Brak. The boy was also smiling but his smile was seemingly fixed in place, and he only looked where the man's hand directed his head. This man whispered into the boy's ear who, acting as an interpreter, spoke up while the man continued holding onto his neck.

'We come to this camp in peace. We are a scouting-party for our tribe, seeking out new lands to settle. We only ask if you will kindly feed us and let us stay with you this night, for we will be on our way come the morning.'

With that, the man holding the boy released him and stepped forwards with a broad grin to clasp Brak in greeting, but something in the way that Brak looked at him stopped him in his tracks, to hold out a hand of friendship instead. Brak ignored the proffered hand and asked,

'Your tribe, where are they, are they close by?'

The man looked at Brak with an open, honest, gaze and then at the boy who told him of Brak's question. Then he spoke to Brak in a way that seemed to the listening Grovi to be both sincere and a little sad. The boy translated for him.

'I am Wolfrem and I regret that our tribe is faraway to the south and the west. It is a long time since we have seen our families, we miss them, but we cannot return to them until we have found new lands to settle.'

Brak was curious who this boy was, and how one who spoke the language of the Grovi came to be with this band of men.

'Tell me boy, how came you to be with these men, tell me true, for they do not understand what we say. Are you their prisoner, or are you with them?'

Wolfrem sensed that Brak was making enquiries directly to the boy and once more resumed his hold on the back of the boy's neck. When the boy spoke, his voice was strained.

'These men found me alone in the wilderness, they fed me, taught me to speak their language and now look after me as one of their own. I am happy to be with them.'

Brak nodded and looked upon the men, trying to weigh them up. Although they were only five men, they were a formidable group. Men in their prime, well muscled and fed. But, if the boy spoke true, they were not a threat to his tribe. Being greatly outnumbered and without their weapons, there would be no harm in letting them shelter in the camp this night. However, he wanted to delay allowing the men into the long-house for as long as possible, so he turned to his men and ordered that a fire should be lit in the centre of the camp, and that a meal should be prepared to honour their guests. While this was being done, he sat on one side of the tusk and beckoned for Wolfrem to sit by him on the other side. Bringing the boy with him, Wolfrem sat and smiled about at all, including at the boy, while together they watched the fire being prepared. Wolfrem's men assisted in building the great fire, going off to the forest with Brak's men to drag back large branches of wood. Brak took the opportunity to ask more about his visitors.

'I am Brak and I am the chief of this tribe, we call ourselves the Grovi. Tell me more about your men and your tribe while we wait, why are you so far away from your tribe and who protects them while you are here?'

He examined Wolfrem closely while he waited for the boy to relate his words. He did not look like a man who had been in the wilderness for a long time, and his manner was more chief-like than he would expect from a man who had been sent out on a scouting mission.

'Well, Brak,' Wolfrem smiled, showing his pleasure at addressing Brak by his name. 'we have killed and eaten most of the creatures where we live and we must soon move on to new lands. My Chief has told me to find such a place, but we have found nowhere so far. We saw people like ourselves in the next valley, so we passed it by to come here, not realising that you were in this valley until we met your women. We are tired and hungry, so thought to come and stay the night with you, hoping that you would be friendly to us. And so you are, we are grateful.'

He paused while the boy related his story and took a measure of how his tale was going down with Brak before going on.

'As for the safety of our tribe, we here are but few but there are many men left behind to keep them safe while we are gone. We are not warlike people Brak, but if we must fight we fight to the death.'

Although Brak was, as Rat always warned him, poor at detecting deception, he could not miss the message the man wanted to convey. Even coming from out the mouth of a boy, this stranger was warning Brak that he was to be taken seriously. Wolfrem pointed to two of his men pulling a particularly large branch towards the fire, and gently shook the boy's neck to ensure that he conveyed his words to Brak.

'Those two are my brothers, Balak and Tilvok, the other two are, well it does not matter what they are called. This boy here,' he smiled at the boy, then waited for him to translate his words before throwing a protective arm around him, 'who I now think of as my son, is called Gaden.'

The boy's face showed some discomfort at being pinned so by the muscular arm, but he managed to convey that he was indeed regarded as Wolfrem's son. While he was listening to Gaden, Brak noticed that Wolfrem and his brothers had blues eyes that gave their expressions a cold look when compared with the brown eyes of everyone else. When the fire was properly alight, Brak asked his men to go into the long-house and bring out food for the guests. It was obvious to all, especially to the five men, that Brak was keeping them away from the women and children. It was not a great feast but plain fair, that filled stomachs and fulfilled all that Brak was obliged to offer to travellers, no more. Afterwards, when all had finished eating and the fire was burning with a low steady heat, Wolfrem, Balak and Tilvok went to stand in front of the fire and sang songs to Brak's men. Although none save their two fellow tribal members and the boy could understand the words, the men sang well and Brak's men were mightily impressed and won over by the harmonies of the brothers. When it was over, there was much cheering and stamping of feet by the Grovi men. The brothers looked about at all the men around them and smiled their appreciation.

When the time finally came to take the men into the long-house, Brak had already had a hearth cleared for them to sit around and sleep. He had ensured that the hearth was not the one nearest the door, but had put two of his best men to sleep in front of that one. He had also sent a man out to hide the weapons laying at the edge of the camp where the men had dropped them. Satisfied that he had done all that he could, he went and joined Culu by his own hearth. She was angry with him.

'What are you doing allowing those men into our long-house with the women and the children? They could attack us in the night.'

Brak did his best to placate her.

'They would be mad to attack us, they have no weapons and we outnumber them. They will be gone in the morning and we will see them no more.'

He went to place his arms around her but she pulled away, she was not content with his answer and glared at him. Brak sighed, knowing that whatever he did she would be in a foul temper until the men had left the camp. He turned to Trovi sitting by the hearth.

'There is a young boy of our race and about your age with the men down there, his name is Gaden, go and make friends with him.'

Trovi was thrilled to meet a boy who was not of his

own tribe, it was a rare event, except when he met the boys from the Salar tribe during the summer-hunting on the plains. So he ran down the long-house, pushed himself between the men and plonked himself by Gaden's side. The boy was about the same height as Trovi but somewhat thinner and without Trovi's already muscular build. Trovi beamed at him and with excitement in his voice said,

'I am Trovi, Brak, the Chief, is my father. Do you want to come sit by my family's hearth and we can play there before we sleep?'

Not waiting for an answer, he grabbed Gaden's hand and pulled him to his feet. Immediately, Wolfrem reached out, placed his hand around Gaden's neck and pulled him back to sit by him once more. Then he leant in and whispered into the boy's ear, who then explained to Trovi,

'I want to stay here, I am tired and I am going to sleep now, sorry.' Then seeing the look of dismay on Trovi's face, added, 'perhaps we could play together before I leave?'

Trovi was hurt, he was not used to being told by

children that they did not want to be with him, his bottom lip came out and for a moment he looked as if he would lose his temper. Then he turned on his heel and stomped away back down the long-house to his father's hearth, to sit with his face cupped in upturned hands.

Brak could see that his son was upset, so he put a hand on his head and ruffled his hair, before wandering down the long-house himself on the pretext of talking to the family sitting by a hearth that was close by Wolfrem and his men. While talking to the family, he was also listening to what the strangers were saying, trying to judge their mood. They seemed happy and were boisterous, speaking loudly, confident that they could not be understood. Although Brak could not understand them, he saw that they were looking at the women and the girls and making comments about them. When he and Rat were children, Rat had tried to persuade Brak to learn his language by teaching him the rudest and most salacious terms relating to women, hoping that such spicy words might pique Brak's interest, to no avail.

However, despite Brak showing no interest in

learning to speak Rat's language, he had remembered some of those words and he was hearing them now, being used about the women of his tribe. He knew men and how they talked with each other about women, but still, hearing his women and girls spoken about in this way made him angry. He thought it best to return to his own hearth before he lost his temper and go to his bed. He had warned all of his men to be vigilant during the night, but he could not sleep and lay listening as the sounds in the long-house slowly quietened until all that was left was the pop and crackle of wood in the fires. He watched all night as the shadows cast by the fires flickered strange shapes around the roof of the long-house, fading to darkness as the fires died down.

Trovi woke just before dawn, pulling on a leather kilt he made his way quietly down the long-house to where the strangers lay sleeping. Stealthily, he reached around Wolfrem and tapped Gaden on his forehead. Gaden's eyes came open to see Trovi reaching down to place his hand over his mouth to keep him quiet. Then Trovi beckoned him to leave the sleeping men and join him. Moving as slowly as he could, Gaden extricated himself from the bodies of his companions and, still dressed as when he had arrived in the camp, joined Trovi as he made his way out of the long-house into the coming light of dawn. He knew that he would be in serious trouble with Wolfrem, but he too wanted to play with a boy of his own age and was prepared to take a beating for it. They made their way to the river, running for the sheer pleasure of it, and when they were far enough away not to be heard began whooping and shouting. Coming to the riverbank, they walked in up to their waists and began to wade down towards the distant beach and the sea.

They played games on the beach, taking turns to run after each other and tackle the one being chased to bring him crashing to the sand. Then they waded into rocky sea-pools, catching crabs and throwing them at each other. It was all magical for Gaden, as he had never seen the sea before and crabs seemed to be remarkable creatures. Eventually, they became tired and breathless and lay side by side on the beach to regain their breaths before returning to the camp. Gaden became solemn; he came to a decision and, taking a deep breath, he turned over onto his stomach to look Trovi in the face and tell him what Wolfrem and his men were planning for the Grovi.

Later, as Trovi and Gaden approached the long-house once more, Gaden started to tremble with fear, knowing why, Trovi put an arm around his new friend and promised that he would do all that he could to ensure that he was kept safe in the coming time of danger. They entered the long-house together and Gaden went up to Wolfrem to explain where he had been, but the words died in his mouth as Wolfrem seized him by the throat with one hand and squeezed until the boy's legs buckled beneath him. The tribe saw what was happening and Brak and several men rose to their feet, Trovi leapt forwards and grasped Wolfrem's wrist with both of his hands to stop him, but Wolfrem continued to hold onto Gaden's throat as his body jerked about in spasms, then just before the boy lost consciousness he was released to lie still on the floor. Wolfrem looked about the long-house with a beaming smile.

'Boys eh, never do as they are told do they?', his men laughed.

The Grovi watched on in silence. Brak walked slowly down the long-house to stand before them, nodding to each man, he spoke to Wolfrem.

'You will be wanting to be on your way no doubt. Come outside and my men will bring food to take with you.'

There was no translation from Gaden, who lay motionless on the floor, but Brak had mimed along with the words and the men seemed to understand his meaning. With a final nod to each, he left them there and went outside into the sunshine. Eventually, Wolfrem and his men came out, Gaden standing shakily by Wolfrem's side and held once more with a hand on the back of his neck. Again, Brak wondered about this boy and what his true role was with this band of warriors, he was sure now that Wolfrem felt no love for him as a son. He sent a man to collect the men's weapons from their hiding place and to place them once more at the edge of the camp, then each man was given some food to take away with them. Wolfrem came to stand before Brak, each taking their measure of the other. Wolfrem spoke and Gaden repeated his words in a tremulous voice.

'You have dealt with us with true honour and hospitality, we thank you.'

This time he knew better than to offer to clasp Brak but instead raised his palm in a farewell gesture and strode off, each of his men raised a hand in salute as he passed and when they reached the edge of the camp they loaded themselves once more with their weapons and disappeared into the forest.

As soon as the last man had vanished from sight, Trovi ran to his father and blurted out the true intent of Wolfrem and his men.

'Gaden is *not* their friend, he is their slave, as is his mother. She is with the rest of Wolfrem's tribe, hidden from sight on the high ridge, forbidden to light fires. Wolfrem is going now to collect his men and return to this camp before tomorrow's dawn; they will kill all the men, the children and the old, only some women will be allowed to live, to become slaves. Gaden warned me of this when we were playing by the sea, he held his tongue in the camp because Wolfrem had warned him that if his men did not return to the tribe his mother's life would be forfeit.'

Shocked as he was by Trovi's revelation, he felt pride that his son was showing no fear at this threat to his life. He obviously had every confidence that his father would save the tribe, but Brak was not so sure, he did not even know how many men that Wolfrem would be bringing when he returned to attack the camp. The one advantage that he had was time, he had all this day and the night to prepare for the coming battle. He ordered that no one was to leave the camp without his permission, and that all weapons were to be sharpened and made good. When asked by his men what they were preparing for he told them that he would tell them when the sun was at its highest.

Then he sent scouts up to search the high forest below the ridge, to make sure that Wolfrem had not posted men to watch the camp: he needed Wolfrem's men to remain on the high ridge, unsighted from what was taking place in the camp. He went and stood by his tusk and folded his arms around it, closed his eyes and thought how he could save his tribe from annihilation. He stood like that for the whole of the morning, even when Culu came to offer him a drink he did not answer but stayed silent and unresponsive.

As the sun reached its zenith, he opened his eyes and looking about saw that the whole tribe was seated about him, waiting for him to speak and to tell them what they had been preparing for. He felt some reassurance to see that his men were in good shape, but although they were good hunters, neither he nor they had ever been tested in a fight for the life of the whole tribe against such a formidable foe as Wolfrem and his men. He knew that this was the defining moment for himself to be a great chief for his tribe; his strategy would need to be perfect and he must now inspire his tribe to be confident that he could save them.

'Listen very carefully to me, if you do exactly as I say then there may be a chance that most of this tribe will sit once more by this tusk at this time tomorrow. Before the next dawn's light those strangers who we fed and gave shelter to will return with many more men and seek to kill us all. If we do not work together then the Grovi may cease to exist when tomorrow night falls on the camp, others will sit by your hearths and sleep in your beds. I will not allow this to happen.'

There was shock and panic on the faces around him, they started talking to each other and gesticulating. He held up a hand to silence them, then pointing to the old men and women,

'You old ones must collect and prepare as much food as you can this day, so that we can feast our fill tonight, for we do not know when we will eat again.'

Then he turned his attention to the rest of the tribe.

'Everyone else, including the children and those mothers with babies on their backs, bring many baskets and follow me, we also have much work to do.'

Except for the old ones, the whole tribe formed into a column behind Brak and Culu and made their way out of the camp and down to the sea. Once there, Brak instructed them all to pick stones from the beach that would fit comfortably into the palms of their hands, even the children must do this, for all would be fighting for their lives tomorrow. When the baskets were full, the men carried them up a steep slope that eventually flattened out on the high cliff-top that overlooked the now deserted seal colony. The land up there was grass-covered and smooth, but a short spear's throw away was the edge of the forest and it was here that the men tipped out the stones into piles. Again and again the baskets were filled and carried up to the cliff-top to be heaped in spaced-out piles along the edge of the forest.

When Brak was satisfied that sufficient stones were stored there, the whole tribe was told to follow him into the forest, where he ordered everyone to cut down branches as long and as stout as they could each comfortably lift. When they had all selected one for themselves, he had them use their axes to trim them smooth and to have a long sharp point shaped at one end. Brak then marked two trees at some distance apart from each other and had the tribe go to stand in a line behind the trees, from one marked tree to the other. Where possible, he had families standing together, for a mother and father would fight all the harder to keep their children away from death.

'Where you stand now, is where you will stand tomorrow morning, mark your spot well and take and pile your own stones in close reach.'

When that was done, they once more formed up in a column and returned to camp. The scouts returned and reported that all was quiet on the ridge, Wolfrem and his men must be resting for the coming fight. Brak told everyone that they should eat now, lightly, as the best should be saved for the main meal tonight. After they had all eaten, he had the axes re-sharpened, and as there was plentiful daylight to work by until late in the day, he had the men and women set about making the light hunting spears, spears that could be delivered with devastating force when used with a throwing stick to notch at one end. By the end of the day, every man and many women, including Culu, had a sharp axe and many throwing spears. It would have to be enough, there was nothing more to be done.

Brak commanded that a great fire be lit once more in the centre of the camp and that every scrap of food was to be brought to the fireside and eaten by all. When they were done and everyone had eaten their fill and more, Brak led them all in singing war songs, love songs and then the old songs of distant lands and lost loves, that caused some of them to weep quietly to themselves. Some wept for the sadness of the songs, but some also wept because they knew that this might be their last night to be alive, singing songs by a campfire with the family that was their tribe.

As the fire died down to a dull glow, Brak went and spoke with each family in turn, everyone must know what they had to do when the time came for fighting. When he had finished, he hugged Trovi and then Culu and told her that he would be relying on her split-second timing to save his life when the special moment would come, he knew that she would not let him down. Culu then called the tribe to follow her down to the beach, where they would climb up to cliff and hide in the forest there. There could be no lights to guide the way, but a full moon offered sufficient light for them to make their way easily enough. Brak stayed behind with two of his strongest and fastest hunters to hide in the forest at the edge of the camp.

Without any weapons, they lay under bracken all night until a faint dawn light started to show in the valley, soon they could make out the outline of the long-house. One of the hunters nudged Brak's side, then slowly pushed a hand out of the bracken to point to the forest's edge on the far side of the camp. Brak peered into the gloom and could just make out the dark shapes of men moving out of the trees and into the camp. More and more men left the forest and made their way silently across the clearing towards the long-house where they clustered in front of the doorway. There was a long pause, then much screaming and whooping as the men stormed into the doorway expecting to find Brak's tribe fast asleep in their beds and easy to slaughter. Then silence fell across the camp.

Inside the long-house, Wolfrem and his men were jubilant, they had been expecting a short but bloody fight, but they found no one in the long-house, it had all been so easy. Wolfrem spoke with his men.

'Gaden must have warned them about our attack and they have deserted their valley. He will suffer for this when I see him again. Still, we now have a new camp and a place where we can make a life for ourselves again, how is that lads eh?'

There was a loud cheer from all the men that Brak and his companions could hear from where they hid. Wolfrem threw himself down on Brak's bed, and Balak and Tilvok went to sit by the hearth.

'Make yourselves at home boys, get these fires going and rest awhile before we bring our women and children to be here with us.'

While Wolfrem posted guards at the four outside corners of the long-house, the other men picked out hearths and sat by them; fires were stoked up and soon the long-house was bright with light from all of the fires. Wolfrem signalled to his brothers to lean in while he whispered to them.

'This is not like Brak, he seemed a proud man to me. Too proud to give everything up without a fight, something is not right here.'

Then he lay back on Brak's bed and wondered what Brak might have planned for them. Outside it was growing lighter, soon everything was clear to the watchers beneath the trees. They could see the guards standing at each corner of the long-house, keeping a vigilant watch all about them. Brak reached out and tapped the man to his left, then reached out and tapped the man to his right. They made themselves ready, drawing deep breaths, then together the three men stood and walked out of the tree-line to stand in full view of the guards.

The first guard to see them called out the alarm, and soon men began running out of the long-house to see what the shouting was about. Brak and his men moved back to hide behind the trees once more. There was much agitation and pointing to where Brak and his men had been seen. Those who were not already armed hurriedly went back in to their hearths to pick up their weapons. Brak saw Wolfrem appear in the doorway and start shouting orders to his men. As one, Wolfrem's men, now all heavily armed and led by Balak and Tilvok, began to run towards the forest. Wolfrem shouted after them,

'Be sure to take one alive, I want to know what Brak is up to.'

Then he returned to Brak's hearth and sat down on the bed. It was as he had suspected, Brak was not going to leave the valley without a fight.

The three Grovi watched as Wolfrem's men grew closer, then Brak gave the command for his men to run, making sure that he was the last of the three to leave. He wanted to control the pace of the chase, not to run so far ahead that the pursuers would give up, nor so fast that the line of the men following would be stretched out too much. He knew every pebble, rock, tree and indentation in the land of this valley, so he did not have to look down to run, he could look back often to keep the distance to the nearest pursuer how he had planned it. The three of them ran along the river bank, following it to the beach then up the incline heading towards the cliff-top. They were very tired but they had the benefit that they were not carrying weapons, unlike their pursuers who were heavily armed and even more tired and breathless than the men they were hunting. There were times when Brak allowed the nearest man, Balak, to get so close to his back that he could hear him panting for breath.

Brak and his men arrived at the cliff-top and ran along its edge, to their left they could see the sudden drop-off to the sharp rocks far below. Brak checked to his right where the first marked tree showed where his hidden tribe began; a quick look back and he saw that Wolfrem's men were strung out in a line, also running along the edge of the cliff. Balak was very close, too close. When he saw the second marked tree that showed where his beloved Culu was waiting with her hunting spear already notched onto the throwing stick, he stopped dead; blocking the way forwards and allowing his two men to run ahead, to double back behind the trees and pick up their own weapons. Weaponless, he turned to face Balak who had also stopped in his tracks. Behind Balak was Tilvok and the line of Wolfrem's men that had now all stopped running to avoid colliding with the man in front of them. Drawing back his axe, Balak swung at Brak, Brak stepped back but because they were so close the blade of the axe sliced across the skin of his chest causing blood to run down his body. His attacker was thrilled to have Brak at his mercy now, without weapons he would be dead in moments.

Suddenly, Brak thrust his hands palm outwards towards Balak, causing him to pause in his next axe swing to wonder what this man thought he was doing. At this moment, Culu stepped out from behind her tree and launched the hunting spear. Precisely aimed with her left hand and driven with great force by the throwing stick in her right hand, it shot across the short distance to pass entirely through Balak's neck. Still holding his axe ready to swing at Brak, he seemed surprised at what had happened to him. His free hand came up to his neck and grasped the shaft of the spear. He stood there looking at Brak, not understanding how this came to be. Then Brak stepped forwards and spoke into his face,

'Here, I can help you with that.'

With one hand he grasped and took the man's axe, and with his other hand he clamped the man's hand onto the shaft of the spear, then spun him around in a circle to release him at the edge of the cliff. Balak took two staggering sideways steps then vanished over the edge. Tilvok was shocked at what had happened, one moment his brother had Brak at his mercy, in the next he was gone. Brak's entire tribe then stepped out from the trees and fired their weapons. The men and some women rained hunting spears into them, while the children and the remaining women threw their stones with all the force they could muster. Brak smiled to himself when he saw that Tilvok had turned his head away to see where this attack was coming from, this was too easy.

Almost casually, Brak swung the axe and destroyed his skull, feeling the man's blood splatter onto his face. Looking down the line, he could see that the two men who had run ahead of him to this spot had picked up their weapons, and now reappeared behind the line of Wolfrem's men to block off their retreat. Halfway down the line of his tribe, he could see little Suffi, the girl that Rat had brought to be adopted by the Grovi, her long black hair swinging backwards and forwards as she hurled stones at the men on the cliff-edge. Standing side-by-side with her was her normally gentle stepmother, Nolly, her face now contorted in rage as she joined with Suffi to drive these men to their deaths. Wolfrem's men had nowhere to escape to, every man had soon been struck by the hail of stones and pierced by hunting spears. Brak roared out,

'Charge.'

As one, the whole tribe hefted their sharpened branches and ran towards the men on the cliff-edge, few of whom were still standing, most now on their knees. Wolfrem's men were driven, screaming in terror and pain, over the edge of the cliff. Soon it was over, after all the screaming and shouting silence fell; the tribe moved together to peer over the edge of the cliff to see the broken men on the rocks below. The tide was coming in, the sea tugging at the bodies, soon to carry them away to sink into the deep water. A cry went up when a man was seen just below the edge of the cliff, he was clinging on with both hands to a rocky outcrop, staring up into the faces of the watching Grovi. Brak shouldered his way through to look down on him, he called Trovi to him.

'Here Trovi, see this man. He would have seen our tribe die today and your mother and the other women taken into slavery. What shall we do with him, shall we pull him up to life, or send him to his death?'

Trovi nodded to the bloody axe that Brak was holding and held out his hand for it. Brak offered him the shaft of the axe and then Trovi lay down on the cliff-edge for his father to take him by his ankles and lower him down to the man. Trovi found himself looking straight into the man's brilliant blue eyes and saw his mouth babbling for mercy. Trovi's face was impassive as he watched the man, then he brought the axe down on one of the man's hands. Screaming in pain and terror, his broken hand dangled by his waist as he still desperately held onto the rock with his other hand. Trovi then brought the axe down on the man's remaining hand and watched him fall, pedalling his legs in his terror, to be shattered on the rocks below. Brak pulled him back up to stand by his side. The whole tribe raised their weapons and spontaneously ululated their joy at being alive and victorious over their enemies. It was an astounding victory, not one member of the tribe had been killed and the only one to suffer an injury was Brak, but the slice to his bloody chest was not life-threatening and would be stitched when they returned in triumph to camp.

They slowly made their way down to the beach and followed the river back to walk into the centre of the camp; they were weary now that the fight was over. Wolfrem had not been among the dead, he could still be in the long-house, so Brak had warned them to remain silent. When they reached the tusk he held up his hand to have them wait there, then dropped his axe and walked into the doorway of the long-house. Wolfrem was sitting and staring into the flames in the hearth when he heard someone enter, beaming with pleasure he turned to greet one of his brothers. The smile died on his face when he saw that it was Brak who was standing there. Brak walked down the length of the long-house and sat opposite Wolfrem. They stared at each other, Wolfrem was very pale beneath his long black hair and beard. Eventually, he turned away from Brak's gaze to stare once more into the flames. Brak saw him gulp, then, still not looking at Brak, he spoke in a voice that was no longer a confident boom but more like that of an old man begging for food.

'My men,' he paused and gulped once again, 'my men, where are my men?'

Wolfrem looked at him to hear an answer. Although Brak did not understand Wolfrem's words, he could guess, so, holding his hands out in front he swept them through a large arc to indicate 'all', then drew his thumb across his neck to show 'violent death'.

Wolfrem's face betrayed his shock and a deep sigh escaped from him. On the walk back to camp Brak had thought about what he would do with this man. If he had been caught with his men and his brothers he would have been killed, either in battle or executed soon after, but Brak now realised there were others to consider. Standing, he beckoned Wolfrem to follow, the beaten chief looked up, resigned to his certain fate, death would be waiting for him outside. As they stepped out of the long-house and the tribe saw that Wolfrem stood there with their Chief, they shouted out in anger and seized their weapons to kill him, but Brak stood in front of Wolfrem and held up his hands for silence.

'I know why you are angry and want to kill this man. We gave him food and shelter, yet he came to destroy us all. Do not forget though, there are women and children up there on the ridge,'

He stopped and pointed to his tribe's women and children.

'Who are just like our own and will surely die in the coming months without some men to protect them. I will take this man to his tribe and let him try to save those that he can. I also seek the boy who saved this tribe, Gaden, so that he can make a home with us, no longer a slave.'

Although he sought to be merciful, he told his tribe that if he was not back by nightfall they were to hunt down Wolfrem's remaining tribe and destroy them all. Then he selected six of his warriors to accompany him and Wolfrem up onto the ridge. Wolfrem began to realise that he was not to be killed, but he no longer cared, he was a broken man, he had failed his tribe. No one spoke during the climb and eventually they walked through the high piles of stones that surrounded the flat ground in front of a cave. When his tribe saw Wolfrem they all cheered in triumph and his woman and his children ran to greet their victorious Chief. Then they realised that the heavily armed men with him were strangers, not of their tribe, their Chief was not a victor but a prisoner of these men. There were sighs and mutterings and some women started to cry, where were their men? The four older men who had been left behind to guard the women and children raised their weapons ready to attack and free Wolfrem, but he raised his hands and stopped them. Brak stepped forward and looked around the semicircle of women and children and bellowed out,

'Gaden, come here boy.'

The centre of the tribe opened up and behind them

could be seen the mouth of the cave, out of which stepped Gaden, blinking in the bright light of the sun. Brak called out to him.

'Bring your mother as well boy, you are coming with us.'

Gaden disappeared back into the cave and returned holding the hand of a woman who looked older and thinner than she should. Together, they made their way through the ranks of the tribe to stand in front of Brak.

'Gaden, you saved my tribe, for that you and your mother will always have a home with the Grovi.'

Gaden beamed his happiness, jumping up and down and jerking excitedly on his mother's arm to make her realise that their torments were now over. Brak held him by his shoulders to quieten him and gave him his last duty for Wolfrem, that he should translate what Brak now had to say. Brak stood before Wolfrem and looked him in the eyes while he spoke, then listened as Gaden translated his words.

'We gave you food, we gave you shelter, then you came to destroy my tribe and to take the valley from us. You have paid a mighty price. I was going to execute you but,'

He waved his arm across the line of women and children standing before him and spoke directly to them again, then waited and watched as Gaden spoke to see what effect his words were having.

'If I had done that, I would have also condemned everyone standing here now to death. Even so, I doubt that with just five men you will be able to survive as a tribe, but I am giving you this last chance for life. You are to leave these lands. Do not go for help to the Salar in the next valley, they are our allies and I will send warning that you are not to be trusted.

He turned back to Wolfrem.

'Have you anything to say before I banish you from the north?'

Gaden translated Brak's words to Wolfrem then gave his reply.

'I had no choice Brak. Your valley was the furthest north and every valley we came to had a tribe living there. My tribe needed your valley and if it had not been for this boy.' Wolfrem pointed to him as Gaden repeated the words. 'My woman and I would be sleeping in your bed tonight and my tribe would have a home at last. We will perish if we do not soon find a land to live in, all hope is gone for us now.'

Wolfrem was in despair and could barely speak, for his anguish was overwhelming. Brak felt some pity for the man and wondered what he would have done in his place. He knew that his own ancestors had done exactly as Wolfrem had tried to do. They had taken food and shelter from a tribe that were living happily in the valley, then repaid their kindness with betrayal and killed them all. There was nothing more to be said. Brak turned away from Wolfrem and his tribe to return to his camp, Gaden and his mother followed behind with Brak's warriors. As he was about to leave the clearing, Brak turned back pulled Gaden to him and spoke in his ear, Gaden shouted the translation back to Wolfrem.

'Be gone by midday tomorrow, or your tribe will face annihilation.'

It was early evening when the small party entered the camp; Gaden received a great welcome from all the Grovi, for every man and woman knew that they owed their lives to this small boy. Brak took the boy and his mother into his family and Gaden grew to be a brother to the boy Trovi, who had once been his friend. Wolfrem and his remaining tribe disappeared into the wilderness and were never seen again.

15

A JOURNEY

When Rat woke he saw that Brak was sleeping, so he put stones on the fire to heat water, then went outside to re-sharpen their axes. While he worked he looked down the valley and out to sea; the sky was clear without a cloud to be seen. This was a good day for them to leave this valley. Unknown to Rat, he was looking in the wrong direction, far inland, beyond the valleys, enormous black clouds were massing over the mountains. By the time he returned to the long-house the stones were hot, so he made a hot drink for them both. He took Brak's drink and sat heavily on his bed. He spoke briskly.

'Wake up friend, we are leaving this valley today. I want you to drink this, then you will eat some meat, you will need all of your strength to climb to the high ground.'

Brak grunted, opened his eyes and turned to face Rat, who was concerned to see that Brak looked bewildered, as if he was not fully aware of where he was, or if he even recognised his friend. He spoke, not as if to Rat but to himself.

'I am Brak, great Chief of the Grovi. I rule in this valley with my woman, Culu. Enemies fear me and friends would die for me,' then softly, 'I am Brak.'

He closed his eyes. Rat placed his arms around Brak and leaned down to whisper in his face, gently shaking him while he spoke.

'I know who you are you old fool. Come back to me, I am Rat your friend.'

Brak opened his eyes again, gazing at Rat's face so close to his own, some recognition seemed to come to him.

'Rat?'

'Yes, Rat. Come on Brak.'

He moved his hands to Brak's back and lifted him gently to sit him up. Sitting now side by side, Brak was bent forward with sagging shoulders, his arms hanging by his side. Reaching behind himself, Rat picked up the drink, then placed an arm around the back of Brak's neck. With his other hand he brought the bowl to Brak's lips, using his fingers under his friend's chin he pushed his head back, then pulled his mouth open. Slowly at first, he poured the drink into Brak's mouth and was relieved to see him swallowing the hot liquid. When most of the drink was gone, he went and fetched some cooked squirrel meat and fed small pieces to his unresisting friend, the way that a mother would feed her baby. He poured the last of the drink into Brak's mouth, then standing, reached down and took Brak's wrists in his hands, stepping back he pulled him to his feet. Brak stood there unsteadily, swaying backwards and forwards, peering into Rat's face as if he was again trying to work out who this man was. Still holding Brak's wrists, Rat bent towards him to speak to him.

'Stand there, do not sit down again.'

He released his hold on Brak's wrists and, keeping an eye on him all of the time, began to dress him as quickly as possible. He slipped an axe into Brak's belt, then a knife but did not give him his spear, they would have to leave without it. He hung two sacks of supplies around his neck, then placing his hands on his shoulders he pushed him back onto the bed.

'Sit there for a while, do *not* lie down.'

Brak sat, then started to lean backwards, Rat caught him with one hand gripping Brak's beard and shouted in his face.

'I said, do not lie down! Sit!'

He released Brak, who straightaway fell back to lie on the bed with outstretched arms. Rat sighed, then bustled about the long-house, getting dressed for travelling and packing sacks to hang around his own neck. When he was fully dressed he put on his shaman's cloak and slung the mask around his neck, then he filled bladders with water and placed them in the remaining sack of cooked squirrels. He added this sack to his already heavy burden and was ready to go. His deformed leg was aching painfully from the effort, and he could only hope that it would not slow him down too much while climbing to the top of the ridge, before descending into what had been the Salar's valley and the safety of Rat's round-house. This was going to be a perilous journey, so Rat decided to take a moment to pray to the Earth Mother for protection. He put down his baggage on his bed and knelt by the dying fire.

'Earth Mother, I ask for your protection today, we need you to watch over us on the journey ahead. If we face danger we will fight but my friend is not well, there is no fight left in him. I ask that you come to our aid if we meet danger. If we make it safely to my valley then I promise that I will dedicate my next sacrifice to you.'

He thought of how he missed the reassurance of the little statue of the Earth Mother that he had given to Suffi when the tribe left the valley. Always kept by the Shaman of the tribe, it had been giving protection to the tribe long before the times that could be remembered. He remained kneeling there, struck by the enormity of what he was trying to achieve. He did not know how he could possibly get Brak up to and across the ridge, and what dangers they might face on the way, he felt weak, old and very afraid.

Gathering himself together, he went and stood with his hands on his hips in front of the prone body of Brak. He sighed a deep sigh, leaned over Brak to remove the sacks from his shoulders, then he seized the front of his clothing and with great effort pulled him to his feet. With one hand steadying Brak, he used the other to pull the sacks from the bed and once more drape them over Brak's shoulders. He quickly put his axe and knife in his own belt before picking up his sacks from the bed; throwing them over his shoulders he then bent down and picked up his spear. He moved backwards to stand in front of Brak.

'Put your hand on my shoulder friend and we will soon find ourselves standing on that high ridge.'

When Rat felt Brak's broad hand on his shoulder he stepped forward and with relief found that Brak was following him down the length of the long-house. Then Brak stopped and turned to place his hands on a mammoth bone that was set into the wall, the bone that he had carried here after he and Culu had returned from the summer-hunting as a couple. Rat allowed him to stand there for a moment, saying goodbye to his past, then went and gently took him by the elbow. Brak did not resist but turned and followed once more. As they left the doorway Rat took the wolf-spear from where it was standing against the wall. He looked over his shoulder to find Brak staring straight ahead, so he allowed them to walk by Sonty's charred remains and towards the standing tusk. When they reached the tusk, Rat turned around to Brak and took one of his wrists in his hand and guided Brak's hand onto the tusk.

'Say goodbye to your tusk old man; I doubt we will see it again, whatever befalls us.'

Brak put his other hand on the tusk also, then ran his fingers down from below the tip to the base where it was fixed into the ground. He could feel scratches deep into the surface. He turned and looked at Rat.

'It is scratched, these scratches were not here before.'

He shook his head in wonder. Then he placed his whole body against the tusk; resting his cheek against it with eyes tight shut. He wrapped his arms around it as if he was holding Culu and a lifetime of memories with her for the last time, Rat let him stand there awhile, then went and placed his hands on his shoulders. He spoke quietly in his ear.

'Come my friend, we must go, we must be over the ridge before the light starts to fade.'

Brak's arms fell to his side, he sighed then pulled himself together. He turned to Rat, who saw the sadness in his face at having to leave his life behind in the now desolate and lifeless valley. Suddenly, Brak stepped forwards and threw his arms around Rat to hug him as he had the tusk. Rat was taken aback, Brak had never shown affection to anyone except Culu and the small children of his tribe. He was also surprised at the strength of Brak's embrace, he could hardly breathe, he was glad he had never had to fight this man. He put his hand on Brak's back and patted him, neither man spoke, then Brak released him but still they said nothing. Rat turned around and Brak placed his hand on his shoulder once more. With Rat leading, his awkward stride rocking him from side to side, they made their way out of the camp and entered the forest.

Behind them, the camp was now forever empty of all life for the first time since the long-house had been built. Inside the house, the last fire to be lit there was dying in the hearth, only one ember was left, glowing a dull red which faded, glowed again, then faded for one last time and went out, a thin spiral of smoke rose up from it to vanish in the air.

Up high in the distant mountains, the clouds continued to build and blacken, deep in their centres flashes of lightning lit their cores before turning black once more. The wind blew stronger, blowing the snow in trails from the mountain tops and slowly pushing the clouds towards the coast. Sunlight once more bathed the mountains, but beneath the moving clouds the land was cast deep in the travelling darkness.

When Rat and Brak left the flat of the valley to ascend to the ridge, Brak had to release Rat's shoulder but still kept close behind the bobbing back of his friend. As they climbed they began to sweat, fully loaded with clothing and baggage the going was hard on the deep snow of the slope. Rat quickly realised that he could no longer carry both the wolf-spear and his hunting spear, the wolf-spear was so long and heavy that he considered leaving it behind. He was stopped from doing so by remembrance of Sonty's death; instead he dropped his spear, and found that he could just about manage the wolf-spear by holding one tip and dragging it alongside them both. They pushed against the tree trunks to lever themselves on, but where the slope became too steep for Brak, Rat would cut steps in the snow with his axe, then climb forward the spear's length for Brak to haul himself, hand over hand, up the shaft of the spear. They had to stop often to rest, Rat was tired but Brak was exhausted, his face was running with sweat and he was gasping to breathe. Rat dropped the sacks from his shoulders, then released the sacks that Brak was carrying.

'We will rest here a while Brak, I am too tired to go on yet. Here, lay back on the snow and rest yourself.'

Brak dropped to his knees, then lay back on the slope and closed his eyes. Rat bent over him and loosened and pulled apart his clothing to cool him down. His breathing was ragged. Rat lay down next to him and they rested, then Rat sat up and cocked his head to listen.

'Brak, can you hear that?'

Brak did not reply.

'The tree-tops are moaning, it will be windy when we leave the trees behind, perhaps it will cool us down eh?'

He took a bladder of water from a sack and drank some, it tasted wonderful. It felt good to be leaving this valley to return to his own and to his round-house. He sat by Brak's head and placed the neck of the bladder to his lips.

'Here, drink this, you will feel better.'

Brak opened his mouth and gulped down the water, then laid his head back down. For the first time since the death of Sonty he smiled.

'Well Rat, we will be sat safe and warm in your round-house tonight. It is many years since I sat with you by your hearth.'

When he thought that Brak had sufficiently rested, Rat stood and offered his hand.

'Come on then old man, let us go. We will be out of the trees soon and the ridge will be in sight.'

They loaded themselves with their baggage. Rat picked up the tip of his wolf-spear and they set off upwards once more; Brak seemed quite recovered and was managing to keep up with Rat. Just when they were tiring again and Brak's breathing was becoming laboured, the trees thinned out and then were left behind. As Rat had predicted, the wind was blowing strong and cold, so they tightened their clothing once more. It was good to see the high ridge now, they would be there soon. Brak sat down on the snow to rest while Rat looked down the valley and out to sea, where he could see that the sky was still clear and blue, then he looked up to the head of the valley and saw enormous black clouds sweeping in, the base of the clouds brushing against the highest parts of the ridge.

As his eyes moved back down the valley he could see four black specks just below the top of the ridge, he could not make out if they were rocks or something else. Then one of the shapes separated from the others and moved towards Brak and himself. It stopped, then the other three shapes moved down to join it. Keeping his head and his body totally still, Rat slowly put his hand down to grasp Brak's shoulder and push down.

'Brak, for your life's sake do not move, we are being

watched.'

Moments passed and he realised he was holding his breath. Gently he started to breathe again in shallow breaths. Brak spoke in a whisper.

'Who is it, are there many?'

Rat did not answer, he was calculating which way to go, down to the camp a long way below, or up to the cave they had discovered as children on the ridge above them. Then the four specks started moving down the slope towards them. Rat gripped Brak's shoulder and pulled upwards. His voice was urgent.

'Get up, we must move now, come, Groden and his pack are heading towards us. We must get to the cave before they reach us.'

They strove up the slope on all fours, Rat leading with his axe in his right hand; there was not enough time to cut steps, instead he struck the axe into the snow and pulled himself up while dragging the wolf-spear in his left hand. Brak was holding onto the other end of the spear and pushing upwards with his legs. Rat looked up and across to check on the progress of the wolves, for a moment he thought that they stood a chance of beating them to the cave, but he groaned when he saw that one of the wolves had separated from the others and was now running at full speed in a straight line for the ridge-top. Up and up they strove and sweated, when Rat looked once again to check on the progress of the lone wolf, he saw that the upper ridge was now covered in cloud and that the wolf had disappeared into the mist.

It turned dark and started to snow, the large flakes driven by the strong wind coated them white. There was a flash of lightning, followed instantly by a deafening rumble of thunder. He checked on the position of the remaining pack, if Brak could keep up they might not catch them in the open. He was tiring and wondered how Brak was doing, but he could not take time to check on him, they must keep going up.

Suddenly, they were in the mist at the base of the cloud, then the ground in front of them started to level out until they were able to stand again and make their way to the mound of rocks that hid the cave. Rat hobbled as fast as he could, Brak holding on to the other end of the wolf-spear was being tugged along. Then to his horror, Rat realised that the end of the spear being held by Brak had been dropped and was dragging along the ground. He turned around and saw that Brak had fallen face down in the snow, running back he pulled him back to his feet. Taking one of Brak's hands in his, and dragging the wolf-spear in the other, he made his way through the jumble of rocks to the flat place where he had lain down as a young boy. Through the falling snow and drifting mist he could see the cave entrance, starkly black against the white snow, they were safe.

There was another brilliant flash of lightning and a simultaneous explosion of thunder, in the dazzling light Rat saw a snowy mound between them and the cave mouth that, as he watched, stood up and shook itself free of snow, it was Roden. Wild-eyed, Rat glanced behind at Brak, to see over his shoulder that Groden and two other wolves were now standing behind them.

'Brak, Roden is between us and the cave mouth, and Groden and his pack are at your back, change places so you can face this bitch down, I will face the pack.'

He brought the wolf-spear up level, tucked under their armpits, then back to back he spun them both around so that Brak was now looking directly at Roden. They stood at the centre of the wolf-spear, holding on with both hands to the spear's shaft, braced against the inevitable attack. Even with his poor sight Brak could recognise Roden at this distance, just beyond the tip of the spear. Rat was angry with himself, he had gambled with both of their lives and lost. Before him Groden was standing with a wolf on either side, and as Rat watched these two started to move out sideways, away from Groden to outflank the tip of the spear. Rat waved his tip from side to side to keep them back, causing Brak to call out in protest.

'What are you doing? She'll get past my end of the spear if you keep moving it, stop!'

Roden's head was lowered and her eyes were fixed on Brak's face, she knew this man, she knew that he could barely see and that he was weak, she could kill him easily. She took a swift bite at the tip of the spear, but was repelled by the smell of the dried wolverine blood and released it. Then she looked past Brak, to fix on Rat's back as he twisted back and forth, this man was a threat to her and her pack. She decided to kill this other man first, and in the moment that she made her decision she leapt to go past Brak and seize Rat. Brak could see her shape change as she crouched to leap and all of his hunting skill came back to him as he took control of the spear from Rat and raised it to meet Roden's leap. The tip of the spear entered the base of Roden's neck and drove deeply into her heart, the force of the impact drove Brak backwards against Rat's back and it was all they could do not to fall. As she died, her sudden weight pulled Brak's end of the spear down, lifting Rat's end of the spear up so that he was standing defenceless, with a wolf in front of him and one on each side. Brak used all of his remaining strength to lift and swing his end of the spear sideways, then suddenly stop so that the body of Roden was flung from the shaft of the spear to tumble into the snow. He gave control of the spear back to Rat, who resumed waving it from side to side to hold back the three wolves.

They were still in mortal danger, the two flanking wolves were now so far apart that it was all he could do to threaten one, without allowing another a clear path through. Brak turned himself around so that he now faced Rat's back and placed his arms around Rat's waist to also hold onto the spear. Groden stepped forwards each time the spear was swung away from him, until when it was swung back he was close enough to catch the tip in his mouth; with a savage bite and a twist of his neck he broke off the tip of the spear. The other two wolves now moved swiftly so that they were almost completely past the men. Still holding the broken spear, Rat saw that it was hopeless, he thought of his prayer to the Earth Mother this morning, and how she had failed to answer him. He was sorry that his friend would die also. Still watching the wolves he turned his head slightly to Brak.

'Goodbye Brak, I loved you like a brother, we are done for, die well.'

Brak had felt the shaking of the spear and heard the snap of the wood above the buffeting wind, then its sudden release, but he was not about to give up. He punched Rat's back, swinging the spear up vertically, he then brought it down and slid the fresh point under Rat's arm towards Groden. He shouted into Rat's ear.

'We fight on Rat, give no ground.'

On top of the cave a shape began to emerge through the driving snow and mist, it was the snow leopard. She stopped at the edge and looked down on the scene below. Groden looked up, saw her and paused in his attack. His companions were unaware of her, and were now in position between the men and the cave. She leapt in a great arc and landed near them, one snarled and rushed her, to be sent somersaulting backwards when her paw smashed into his shoulder. The other wolf looked at her for a moment before retreating back to stand alongside Groden. The wolf that had been struck came unsteadily to stand again before limping away to join the others. Rat was surprised to see that the pack was reforming in front of him, and held the spear as firmly as he could in case they rushed him together.

Behind Brak's back the snow leopard walked slowly forwards, its head held low and with ears laid back against its head, it kept its gaze locked onto Groden, its tail twitching back and forth as step by step it came to stand by the men. If either man had put down a hand, he would have felt the soft fur on the back of the leopard, but their eyes were fixed ahead and their hands were gripping the spear. Groden and the snow leopard were looking straight into each other's eyes. Groden weighed the odds, he could not afford to lose a pack member to this creature; he made his decision and turned away. Followed by his companions he trotted off through the falling snow, almost immediately they vanished from sight. The snow leopard looked up at the men, then turned and ran to the cave, leaping before it to land above the entrance again. She turned and looked down one last time on the men before vanishing back into the mist. Within moments, the falling snow had filled her shallow tracks.

Brak did not know that the wolves had left, and was still bracing himself for an attack when he felt Rat release the wolf-spear, then saw him fall to his knees. Brak stood there holding the spear alone, then he also dropped it to go forward and place his hands on Rat's shoulders. He was not sure what had just taken place.

'Are they are gone? What happened, why did they leave us?'

'I have no idea, we were lost, I expected to die.'

Rat wondered if his morning prayer had saved them, but if so, how the Earth Mother had intervened was a mystery.

'We cannot travel in this storm Brak, we will spend the rest of today and tonight in the cave, and hope for good weather tomorrow.'

He stood and picked up the spear with one hand and took Brak's hand with the other to lead him to the cave.

16

THE CAVE

They had to crouch down slightly to enter the cave, Rat went in first, holding the wolf-spear ahead of him in case there was a bear or other creature using the cave for a winter shelter. Because of the storm it was very dark in there, so Rat pushed and prodded the spear in all directions, finally striking the tip against the back of the cave before he was satisfied that they were alone. They had spent so much time in here as children they could still remember the shape and form of where they were with ease. The roof was too low to stand, so sitting near the back of the cave, they removed their baggage and weapons, then Rat returned to the entrance to build a wall of snow, leaving a small gap for fresh air to enter. It was such a relief to feel safe once more and to be sheltered from the storm.

The snow melted on their furs, so they removed them and turned them upside down for something to lie upon. Brak lay down on his furs while Rat scrabbled through one of his bags, eventually finding and removing a bundle of short bulrush stems that had been flattened at one end and soaked in animal fat. He usually placed these around makeshift altars when he was carrying out ceremonial duties as a shaman, but for now they would provide a meagre light for them. Selecting one candle, he struck his fire-stones until a spark caught on the flat end of the stem, then he blew on it until it a flame grew to provide a little light. He held the flame up to illuminate Brak' face, he did not look well. Sweat glistened in the light, he was gasping to breathe and his eyes had dulled once more. Rat placed the candle in the earth of the floor, reached into a bag and pulled out two cooked squirrels then placed some meat in one of Brak's hands.

'Here, eat this or you will not have strength for our journey tomorrow.'

Brak just lay there, his hand did not curl around the meat; in the faint light Rat could see that his eyes were closed and that he was shaking his head slowly from side to side. When he spoke, his voice was low and weak.

'Not now Rat, I'll eat in the morning, leave me be.'

Rat took back the meat and sat eating, thinking of the day they had first come into this cave. On the day that they had first met on the ridge so many years ago, Rat had pointed to where the cave was and waved Brak to follow him. They had stood side by side in the entrance, Brak having to bend slightly but Rat was then short enough to stand upright. Peering into the beginning of the cave, they wondered what they might find in there. They looked at each other and laughed at their fear, then Rat pushed Brak's elbow to get him to go in first. With his axe held in one hand, Brak had slowly made his way forwards, Rat walking behind him and a little way back. The cave was not large and because the day outside was so sunny there was enough light to see the whole of it.

At the very back they found the bones of a large beast, its skull as big as Rat's chest, and whose eye-sockets seemed to be watching whoever entered the cave. They paid it the respect to be shown to all dead creatures, leaving the bones alone to continue laying there in peace. They scuttled back to the entrance to lie down with their bodies in the cave while their heads poked out to see the flower bedecked ground. When they bent their necks up, they saw the blue sky and moving white clouds. It felt strange to exist in the two worlds of being out in the open with the wind on their faces and in the same moment to be underground.

Suddenly, young Rat jumped to his feet and burst from the cave and ran through the flowers, arms raised he was whooping and laughing in the joy of being young and alive. When he stopped and turned, he saw that Brak was running after him with his arms raised, but also limping with one leg in a mockery of how Rat had just run. The laughter died in Rat's throat and hurt contorted his face, he did not know that Brak had meant no harm, he was just having fun with his new friend.

When they were face to face once more, Brak wanted to say something to ease his pain but they spoke in different tongues. So, with a broad smile, Brak grasped Rat's wrist, and pulling sideways, used his foot to sweep Rat's legs from under him. Rat crashed to the ground with a grunt and rolled face down to hide his tears. Brak was at a loss to know what to do; if he had done this with one of his friends they would be having a play fight now. This boy was reacting more like a young girl.

Brak sat and watched and waited; after some time Rat lifted up his head from his elbow and with a wet face looked at Brak, who smiled at him while crossing his eyes. Rat started to laugh, he realised that this rough boy was not deliberately cruel, like the Salar boys who taunted him for his weakness, and he determined in that moment to make a special bond with this Brak. Also, as young as he was, he knew that he must take every opportunity to develop special skills to increase his value in his tribe. If he could learn to speak with this boy's tribe and learn their ways, he could be of some future service to his Chief.

From that day on, except when Brak was away in the summer on the hunting-plains, they took every opportunity to spend time with each other. At first, they would meet at the cave and play together on the ridge, but one day Brak gestured for Rat to follow him down into the valley of the Grovi. Rat was fascinated to see how different Brak's tribe was from his own: in speech, in clothing and in so many other ways, and he was especially impressed by the long-house, it seemed wonderful that everyone lived together as one huge family.

He would later change his mind; when he was older, less tolerant of others and their ways, then he came to prefer his round-house. The Grovi welcomed him as one of their own, and he was eventually given a bed by the hearth of Brak's family. He quickly learned to speak the language, and the more that he understood what was being said, the more that he could learn from sitting with the tribal elders. Oftentimes as they grew older Brak would go off hunting, so Rat would sit with the old ones, listening to their stories of other, more ancient human tribes and of exotic plants and creatures. There were handed-down tales of long ago, living far south in warm lands, with strange creatures that ran across hot plains, enormous creatures with necks so tall that they could eat from the tops of trees, and of mammoths that were not covered in hair, but naked. Rat sometimes doubted that these creatures could have existed, they seemed so different to all of the creatures that he knew of in the valleys.

The first time that he returned home in the

morning after he had spent the night with the Grovi, his mother was furious with him and slapped his face, then she took him in her arms and cuddled him. She had not slept all night, and was he not aware of the dangers of walking alone in the wild? His father was indifferent, if an animal was to take Rat then he would be happy, his son was a daily embarrassment to him. If his woman had not fought so hard with him to let the baby live, he would have allowed Sabal to take him and leave him in the forest. Unloved by his father and taunted by the boys, Rat felt in many ways more at home with the Grovi than with his own tribe. He knew that his mother was right to warn him about the dangers that he faced travelling from valley to valley alone, but this just inspired him to carefully observe all of the wildlife, especially the local wolf pack. He would not set off unless he knew where the wolves were that day, and they had to be high on the opposite ridge before he would consider setting out for Brak's valley.

He always felt safer when he was with Brak. Even when he was young, Brak gave off an air of self-assurance that made Rat feel confident that his friend could deal with any situation they might find themselves in. For that reason, whenever he was leaving the Grovi's camp, he would sometimes ask Brak to accompany him up to the ridge, and often they would stay for a while by the cave talking with each other. At first it was only by sign language, but as Rat became fluent in the language of the Grovi they could have more animated conversations. There was much laughter and smiles in those days, before Brak became a chief and a renowned hunter and started to take himself very seriously. At first, some of Brak's friends became resentful that he would spend so much time with a boy from a different tribe, but when they got to know Rat better they grew to like him also and would involve him in whatever they were doing. There came a day when they were older but not yet men, when Brak said to him,

'I have been talking with my family and with the Chief, and I have been given permission to ask if you wish to join our tribe and become one of the Grovi, would you want to do that?'

Rat was surprised and honoured that these people would ask him to join them. He did not know what to say, he was very moved. But his tribe would not forgive him if he left them for another tribe, so he would never see his mother again. Also, there was nothing for him to do in this tribe, he could not be a hunter and the Grovi had no gods, so he could never become their Shaman. Brak persisted,

'We know that you are not happy in your own tribe, and that you laugh and smile more when you are with us, so why not my friend?'

'I would be honoured to join your tribe Brak, but there is no use for me here, what would I do? You know that with this leg that I cannot hunt, but I must do useful work if I can. I will be the Salar's Shaman when Sabal has gone to the Earth Mother, I will have some status then. Please tell your family and your Chief that I am pleased that I was asked, and that, if they will allow, I will be as much of a brother to you as I can be while still belonging to the Salar. Will you have me as your brother?'

'Of course Rat, we will always be friends and brothers.'

Rat thought to step forwards and hug him but he knew Brak too well, he would not welcome that at all. Instead he held his hand out and, after a small hesitation, Brak took his hand and squeezed it. And so the friendship continued when they became men, and Brak was Chief of his tribe and Rat was at last the Shaman of the Salar. It had continued until Trovi was taken by the Salar, causing Rat and Brak to fall out for years, until they met once more in the long-house, both men alone, without tribes and without families.

Rat finished the meat and threw the remains towards the back of the cave where the massive bones of the long dead creature lay. He went to the cave entrance and broke away part of the snow wall that blocked the opening, then stepped outside. It was dark now and the storm had moved far out to sea, occasional silent flashes of lightning could still be seen near the horizon. He saw the body of Roden, she looked pathetic in death and he felt sorry that she had to die. He looked up to see that the moon was momentarily covered by a single cloud and cast little light, allowing the countless stars to shine all the brighter in the black sky. It was then that he saw green light dancing across the valleys and up to the sky.

He turned and walked rapidly back into the cave to grasp the furs beneath Brak with both hands. It was a hard pull at first, but he managed to get him moving and succeeded in pulling the sleeping Brak completely out of the cave still laid on his bedding. He rushed back into the cave and retrieved his own furs to lay them next to Brak. He then lay down on his back next to his sleeping friend, seized his face in one hand and gently shook it from side to side.

'Wake up Brak, wake up, look up there, the Earth Mother and our ancestors are dancing across the sky.'

Brak opened his eyes, but all he could see with his blurred vision was the sky faintly changing colour.

'You dragged me outside for this? I have seen these lights many times before when my eyes could see but now, well if she is dancing then she dances for you, not for me, take me back inside before I freeze to death.'

Rat placed the back of one hand on Brak's chest to quieten him, then lay back open-mouthed in wonder at the lights flashing above them, dancing from one end of the sky to the other, changing colours, sometimes green, sometimes purple, blue and violet. Like Brak, he had seen her display herself this way many times since he was a child, but he had never lost the awe of watching his god dancing across the sky. Brak spoke in a quiet voice.

'Do you hear me Rat, take me back inside the cave, I am shivering to death here.'

Rat came out of his reverie and turned his head to look at his friend, they were so close, laid side by side, that he could see the fog of his own breath floating over Brak's closed eyes. He stood and took hold of the furs above Brak's head to pull him easily over the snow back to the cave, where it became more of a struggle to drag him over the earthen floor. He went back outside alone and watched the aurora until he also became too cold, then he picked up his own furs and returned to the cave. Kneeling by Brak he turned him onto his side, then lay down behind him and used some of his own furs to cover them both; throwing an arm over him he cuddled into his back to keep him warm.

It was very dark and quiet in the cave while he listened to Brak's laboured breathing, he thought of the remains of the creature against the back wall and wondered about it dying here alone. Was it watching the morning light spilling into the cave entrance when it took its last breath, or did it pass in the darkness of a never-ending winter night? He fell asleep, to be woken just before dawn by Brak elbowing him repeatedly in the stomach. The first thing that struck Rat, sleeping as he was with his head inside the furs, was the awful smell. Brak turned his head and whispered over his shoulder.

'Rat, I think that I may have shit myself.'

'Oh, you may think that you have shit yourself, I *know* that you have, I can smell it. It is too dark to do anything now, we will wait till it is light. Do not move and do not lay on your back, lie still and try to go back to sleep.'

He pulled his groin back away from Brak and laid his arm over him to hold him still. Brak fell asleep once more and Rat lay with his eyes open, waiting for the light of dawn to lighten the cave. Slowly the cave became lighter, but Rat kept still and allowed Brak to sleep on. This was going to be an important day for them both, they had to get down to his old camp and round-house to be safe once again. He knew that Brak was fading from him and wondered if he could bring him back to be strong enough for the descent down into the valley.

While he held his old friend, he smiled at the remembrance of how young, vital and driven he had once been. One day, when they were young men standing on the beach below the Grovi's camp, Brak had grabbed him by the wrist and ran towards the base of nearby cliffs, forgetting in his haste of Rat's leg, so Rat was forced to hop and jump behind Brak's back to keep up with him. There were thin slabs of rock laying on the beach by the cliff face, Brak went around them looking for one of a suitable size. Finding one, he got Rat to grip one end while he took the other, together they lifted the slab and carried it across and up the beach. It was hard work, the rock was heavy, so they took many rests on the way. When they were up above the height of the highest tide, Brak stopped and lowered his end of the slab, Rat dropped his end in relief and rubbed his arms to relieve the pain.

While they rested, Rat looked at the surface of the rock to see that seemingly carved into it were seashells that were just like the seashells to be found on this beach, but there were also strange creatures that he had never seen before. As he ran his fingers over them he wondered who could have done this, they were so detailed they looked as if they could come to life and move as he looked at them. Rat tried to point them out to Brak, but he was not interested. He had begun to dig a deep trench with his bare hands, looking up and gesturing for Rat to dig also, Rat sighed and decided to humour his friend's strange behaviour. When the trench was deep enough to satisfy Brak, he tipped one end of the slab into it and packed it with stones and sand.

The rock stood waist high to a man and faced the sea, Brak looked very pleased with himself. Rat was dismayed when he found that this was just the beginning of Brak's plan. They were to spend all of that day carrying and erecting slabs of rocks at the top of the beach. When they were finished, standing side by side they brushed the sand from their hands, Brak placed his hands on his hips and beamed at his creation. From a distance it looked as if a crowd of strange human-like creatures were

standing looking out to sea. All day Brak had
refused to answer Rat's questions, so now that they
had finished Rat asked him once more,

'Why have we done this thing? My arms ache and I
have not eaten all day, I am starving. Tell me, what
are these stones for?'

'They are not for anything. They are here because I
made them stand here, this would not exist if I had
not made it so, I have changed the world a little
have I not?'

'Well yes, you change the world when you build a
long-house, but you can eat and sleep in a long-
house, these serve no purpose.'

Brak took one hand from his hip, ran his fingers
through his beard and thought how he could
explain why they were important to him.

'You are right, they serve no purpose at all, except
that they please me to look on them,' he turned and
with a smile looked in enquiry into Rat's face, 'is
that not a good enough reason Rat?'

Rat thought on this then laughed. He slapped Brak
on the back.

'Yes, that is a good enough reason for me, if they make you happy then it was worth the doing. Come let us go and eat.'

Afterwards, whenever they came down to the beach Brak would make a point of going over to stand proudly by his stones, sometimes absently stroking their tops while he looked at them, then looking over to Rat with a proud smile.

Rat remembered him as he was in those days, a man coming into his prime, totally confident but lacking in arrogance, with a powerful physique that Rat envied. His hair would blow gently about his face in the sea-breezes, and his face was always illuminated by the drive and passion that shone from him. A man totally in tune with his world and who took joy from it all.

In contrast, Rat remembered himself to be always feeling alien to this life, something of an outsider, even in his own tribe, never a good fit wherever he found himself, so when he was with Brak he would take the reflected rightness of him, and do his best to emulate it, he always failed. He often wondered what Brak had ever gained in return from being with him, a small, slightly built man, with an awkward manner and a crippled leg. Whatever it was, Rat was grateful that Brak had always, for some unknowable reason, valued his friendship.

There was sufficient light to see by now, so Rat took his arm away from around Brak, and slowly backed out from under the furs. Taking some furs from his bed, he pulled them around himself, went outside and walked to stand on the ridge facing down into his own valley. He watched as a dull red sun slowly rose above the mountain top, seeing the light moving steadily down the valley to blush the snow pink, and finally to illuminate the distant cluster of round-houses far below. He wanted to set off at once, on his own, to go as fast as his leg would allow, to find himself once more at the door of his own round-house, to go inside and start a huge fire in his hearth, driving the cold winter from the home that meant so much to him.

Instead, with a weary heart he reluctantly turned back to go back to the cave, stopping on the flat ground before it to scrape away the deep snow. Beneath the snow, the plants that had flowered with so much colour in the spring and the summer were now just dry grassy stems that he gathered into bundles. He placed two of the bundles under his armpits and carried two more in his hands. When he entered the cave he took a deep breath and went to kneel by Brak's sleeping body. He pulled the furs from him, then rolled him onto his front, taking Brak's chin in one hand he turned his face sideways so that he could breathe. Then he loosened Brak's clothing so that he could clean the shit from his arse. The smell was rank enough that he had to turn away, take a deep breath, then hold it while he returned to his task. One by one, he took the bundles and used them to clean Brak before he put Brak's clothing together once more. When he was finished, he rolled him onto his back and went outside to hurl the bundles as far from the cave as he could.

He stood there a while, breathing deep breaths of the wonderfully cold clean air, then he crouched down and scrubbed his hands clean with snow. Brak had appeared to sleep for the whole of the time it took to clean him, but Rat was not sure if he truly slept, or if such a proud man was too ashamed to admit to being awake while his arse was being cleaned by Rat, as a mother would do for a baby. When he returned, he saw that Brak was awake; Rat smiled at him and the corners of Brak's mouth seemed to move up slightly in a faint imitation of a smile in return. Neither man would mention what had just happened. Rat knelt by Brak's head and, nose to nose with him, spoke quietly but with a sense of urgency.

'Today, when you are recovered, we must go down to my valley. I can let you rest until the sun is high if you need it, but then we will have to leave this cave, will you be up to it?'

Brak, coughed and Rat could smell that his breath was sweet, like rancid honey, he knew that this was not a good sign. He put his hand around Brak's neck and felt for his pulse, it was weak and fluttery. He raised his voice.

'Do you hear me old man, can we leave here today? Answer me.'

Brak brushed Rat's hand away, turned over onto his side and with a sigh fell asleep. Rat wondered if it would be possible to drag Brak down the slope while he still lay on his furs, but he knew that it would not work, it was so steep he would never be able to keep him on the bedding. Also, he was now so weak that Rat doubted he could withstand being jostled and bumped on the trail. Rat went to sit by the skeleton of the large beast at the back of the cave and rested a hand on its broad head while he considered his options. Apart from meat from Roden's corpse, which would have to be eaten raw, they now had only two cooked squirrels left to eat and one bladder of water to drink. Coming to realise how dire their situation was, he wrapped his arms around himself and began to rock backwards and forwards in his anguish.

He closed his eyes tight-shut to escape from where he was and pictured the memory of when he would sit on his bed, listening to the old songs his first woman, Asa, would sing softly to herself during cold winter nights by the hearth. The one that she sang most often was a song of lost love and abandonment.

In the falling days of Autumn

In the dark beyond the fire

In the cold outside the den

In a corner of my heart

Remains a memory of you

We had our Spring together

Felt sure to be forever

But you looked away and past me

Left to feel my loss alone

I swore to forget you and always

Treat future love with scorn

But happy were the days of Summer

Finding love with any other

Everything was there for me

And the centre of my being

Had no memory of you

But in the falling days of Autumn

In the dark beyond the fire

In the cold outside the den

In a corner of my heart

I still find a memory of you

If it were always Summer

I would lie with any other

And never feel the pain

But now Winter lies deep beyond the fire

Bitter cold surrounds the den

And I weep in memory of you

When she would finish the song, there was often a tear in her eye which she would brush away, then laugh at herself for being so foolish, before once more busying herself with chores. He had given it no thought at the time, but sat here now he wondered if there had been a lost love in her life that made her feel so sad, and why had he not noticed her sadness at the time. Whether she had truly loved him or not, he still wished that he was sat now by that hearth with her and his family, to hear her sing softly to herself one last time. If he, Rat, had not been the love of her life, then it struck him that the only two people in his life who had truly loved him were his mother and the man who lay on the cave floor before him. He felt ashamed that he was feeling so angry and frustrated with him for preventing him from going home.

He wanted to weep in pity for himself, but he had no tears left. With Brak drifting away from him, he had never felt so alone. He went over and lay down beside him. He threw an arm over Brak's chest and cuddled into him, more for the comfort of physical contact with another human than it was for the sleeping Brak. While he lay there, he remembered one special night sitting with Brak when they were boys, by the hearth of Deron, the Grovi's keeper of the tribe's history and storyteller. He smiled at the memory that the Grovi and the Salar had much more in common with each other than either tribe would ever know.

17

DERON

In the autumn of the year when they had first met on the ridge, Rat asked Brak to visit his family in the valley of the Salar. Rat had been with the Grovi many times and was made welcome there, so Rat was excited to show his own tribe that he had a special friend. It would have been too dangerous for Brak to enter the valley alone, so first they met on the ridge then made their way to the Salar's camp together. As they walked side by side along the valley to the camp they met a group of women foraging on the edge of the forest. One girl, who did not like Rat, and who never missed an opportunity to make him feel uneasy, shouted out,

'Rat, what are you doing with that ugly creature, are you taking him home to be a slave for your mother?'

The other women and girls laughed, Rat was grateful that Brak had no grasp of his language but Brak knew that he was being ridiculed in some way. He could not understand why he was not being treated with respect. He smiled at the women and raised a hand in greeting, but this was met by more giggling and face pulling. Rat was furious.

'This is my friend you bitches, treat him with some respect!'

The girl who had shouted out laughed and said,

'Silence you little cripple, or I'll come over there and slap you onto your back.'

Brak was now glaring at the girl, so Rat took him by his arm and pulled him forwards.

'Come friend, take no notice of them, we are nearly at my round-house, come on.'

Reluctantly, Brak turned away from the women and resumed walking with Rat. He looked about the camp, bemused that there was no long-house but instead a cluster of separate round-houses, how could this tribe be a tribe if they did not live together? Rat had told his mother that he would be bringing him, so she was expecting them and had prepared a hot meal. She smiled a welcome to Brak, gestured for him to sit by the fire and set the food in front of him. Brak nodded and smiled back, at least one member of this tribe, apart from Rat, was friendly to strangers.

'This is my friend Brak mother, he does not speak our language, although I can speak for him.'

This was the first time that she had been close to one of these different humans, she was intrigued. His clothes were not as well made as those worn by her tribe, but he had an open, honest face and when he smiled his face lit up with his warmth. He was not as handsome as a young Salar man, but he had a powerful physique and a rugged honesty about him that was attractive. For his part, Brak warmed to this woman, but she looked careworn and had a sadness about her that he would never see in a woman of his own tribe. He took up his food, making a point of eating it with relish, nodding and smiling his appreciation to both Rat and his mother. Rat smiled proudly at his mother, he was glad that she had accepted his friend. His mother started to say,

'You are most welcome here Brak, Rat has told me much about...'

But she fell silent as Rat's father appeared in the doorway, placed his spear by the door but kept his axe in his belt. As usual, his face was stern and uncompromising.

'What is this beast of a boy doing sitting by my fire woman?'

He walked forwards, stood directly in front of where Brak was sitting and glowered down on him. Brak looked up and smiled at him, gesturing to indicate that he was enjoying the meal. Rat's mother spoke up in a nervous voice.

'This is Rat's friend from the next valley, he is called Brak. I did not think that you would mind him being here.'

Her voice trailing away to a whisper. His father looked over his shoulder, then turned and stood in front of her. He lowered his head to be nose to nose with her.

'You did not think I would be angry if I return to my home and find this animal sitting by my fire, eating my food? What would make me angry, if not that eh?'

Rat was dismayed that his mother was now in trouble with his father, he had not meant it to be like this.

'It is my fault, I thought that you would want to meet my friend.'

This was a lie, he had expected his father to still be away hunting and had not wanted him to meet Brak, he knew how he would react.

'Your mother should not have allowed him in here, these beasts steal our game and attack our women. We should kill them on sight. Perhaps I should kill this one? I have just cause.'

He pulled his axe from his belt and turned and stood before Brak again. Brak put down the bowl he was eating from and looked up at him, then suddenly he stood, his head level with the man's chin. He took the father's axe wrist in one hand and simultaneously stamped hard on his instep. Then drawing his own axe, he drove the heavy end of the shaft in a powerful blow under the father's chin. He held onto the man's wrist as he dropped his axe, his eyes rolling back in his head as he fell on his knees to the floor, then Brak released his wrist to allow him to fall unconscious onto his back. Brak looked at the mother, then at Rat.

'Rat, say to your mother I am sorry for this, but he pulled his axe on me, I had no choice.'

Although Rat was very pleased with what Brak had done, his mother was holding one hand in front of her mouth and looked shocked at the sudden violence in her home. She went and knelt by her man and took his hands in hers; looking up at Rat, she jerked her head back to indicate that they should leave. Brak understood the gesture well enough, and after nodding in respect to Rat's mother, walked out of the round-house. Rat went over and put his hand on his mother's shoulder.

'Please do not blame Brak, in his tribe a man must never draw a weapon unless he means to use it, he was just defending himself. He is not a bad boy.'

His mother looked up at him, her hands were shaking, Rat could tell that she was fearful for herself when her man came round, perhaps he would he take it out on her. Rat also wondered if his father would make him pay for bringing the 'beast' into the family's round-house. He did not care, he was pleased to see the man who despised him being given a painful lesson in how to fight. He patted his mother's shoulder, then went out of the round-house to join Brak. He was striding off in the distance, so Rat had to hobble as fast as he could to catch up with him. He could see that Brak was furious and looking about angrily, spoiling for another fight. He knew that the boys of the tribe were playing by the river, so he steered Brak away and took a more direct route back to the base of the ridge, otherwise there could have been a bloodbath this day. Once they entered the tree-line and could no longer be seen from the valley, he caught Brak's arm to stop him. Brak whirled around, his face still showing his anger.

'Brak, I am sorry for the way that the girls and my father behaved, you did right. The truth is I am glad that you hit him, he has wanted me dead my whole life. I owe you my thanks.'

Brak was shocked by Rat's words and especially that his father would want him dead, he felt better now about hitting him.

'When we are grown Brak we must end this hatred between the tribes. Together we can do this, just think, many years ahead our tribes could be hunting together on the plains, and defending the valleys as allies, not enemies. It will take time but I think that our friendship could make it happen. When the Grovi and the Salar see that we can be friends, why not them also?'

Brak nodded his understanding of Rat's plan.

'Till this day I did not hate the Salar but your tribe is a hard tribe to love. I hear your words, so if you can work your ways with your tribe I will do the same with the Grovi. But Rat, I will never have an alliance with people who look down on me and my tribe. I would go to war first. Until your tribe respects me and mine, I will not return here. So, my little friend, it is you who will have to visit me, where you know you will be welcome.'

He smiled at Rat, then turned to face the slope and began to bound up at a speed that Rat envied. Just before he disappeared, he turned and waved farewell.

When Rat returned to the round-house his father was sitting in front of the fire staring into the flames. He did not look up or speak to Rat, humiliated as he was by being knocked down by a boy. His mother was sitting on the bed with one hand holding onto her face, Rat suspected that his father had struck her in his shame. When finally his father moved away from the fire, Rat could not help but smile when he saw that the foot that Brak had stamped on was causing his father to walk in the same hobbled way as his despised son.

Brak never returned to the camp, but when both were men, one a chief and the other a shaman, they were able to break down the barriers between the tribes. The hunting was then shared on the plains and, after a meeting of the tribal councils, boundaries for hunting and foraging in the valleys were also agreed, so fighting never took place between the Grovi and the Salar. Brak would not come again to the Salar camp, so Rat was the one who would visit the Grovi; he was happier there for they accepted him as he was. He missed his mother, but Brak's father showed him more respect and care than his own.

If Brak was away hunting Rat would sit down to talk with the tribal elders. One night, when Brak was thirteen summers old and Rat had seen ten, they went to sit at the hearth of Deron, the keeper of the tribal history and the tribe's storyteller. With Deron was one of his sons; it took many years to learn all of the history of the tribe and the various stories to tell it by: so it was the custom that one son of a history-keeper would be selected to sit by his father and memorise them all, for if a tribe lost its history, it lost its identity.

Deron was old now, his beard was grey and his hair was straggly and thinning. With a nose too broad, even for a Grovi, and with eyes that seemed to pop out of their sockets when he was retelling the tales, he was not an attractive man. However, he had the power to capture and hold an audience, whether it was the children of the tribe, or the elders who had heard the stories many times before. As the boys knelt before him, he looked on them and asked,

'Are you here for a story boys? What would you care to hear about eh, think on it, I will tell you only one tonight. What will it be?' He looked from one to the other. Then Rat spoke up.

'Tell us the oldest story that you have, of how the Grovi came to be, will you do that?'

He gave Deron his most earnest and pleading look.

'Well not one thing made this tribe the Grovi, but the oldest time that I can tell you about tells of the Mother of all of the Grovi and how she came to give birth to our tribe.'

Rat leaned forward excitedly.

'The Earth Mother, is that who she was?'

'Boy, to us the Mother is not a god, your god yes, but not ours. No this is the tale of a real woman who pissed and shit like us and who gave birth to us all. Will that story do?'

The two boys nodded. Deron cleared his throat and thought, so long did he stare into his fire that the boys began to wonder if he had forgotten they were there. Then he came to himself and started his story.

'Long, long ago in a land as far away as a place can be there lived a small tribe of humans. This was a hot land, there was no ice or snow there, so these people wore no clothes and walked about as naked as babies.'

The boys looked at each other in disbelief.

'They had once lived far from the sea but had come over time to live by a rocky shore. They were there for a hundred summers, and although at first they had feared the sea, they came to live with it for it gave much food for the men and women brave enough to enter its waters. This sea was a dangerous place, with poisonous creatures and giant fish and monsters that would take a man if he went into deep water. Their bodies could never be found to be given a farewell by their family, they would vanish forever.

When the tribe had first arrived in this place there was fresh water and there were trees and many plants and animals to feed upon, but over many years the desert that they had crossed to reach this place began to move towards the shore. The trees and the plants began to die and fresh water became hard to find without digging into the earth. The Chief of this tribe, I shall call him Man, knew that something must be done or the tribe would perish. He also knew that the desert, that had been almost too wide to cross those hundred summers ago, would be impossible to cross now. They were trapped and would surely starve to death.

Looking out to sea, in the distance could be seen new land that, even from far away, looked green and welcoming. There were now no trees to cut down and bind together to float to that land, they would have to swim. When he told the tribe of his decision to go to that place there was much distress, no one wanted to swim so far and how would the young children and babies get there? There was murmuring of dissent, until finally one man was pushed forward to tell their Chief that they would not go, they would stay on this shore and take their chance that the desert would in time retreat back again. Man knew that he could not drive his tribe into the sea, but he would not stay here to die of thirst or hunger. It was agreed that he would go with his woman. Deron smiled at the two boys.

'What shall we call this woman with Man?'

Together they shouted back, 'Woman!'

'Alright,' he nodded slowly, 'Woman it is then. Well, Woman was prepared to take the long swim with Man and also Man's brother and his woman would go with them.'

He stopped and raised his eyebrows, asking the

question.

Rat called out,

'His brother was called Brother!'

Brak laughed and shouted,

'And her name was Brother's Woman!'

'Very good,' said Deron, slapping his knees, 'these shall be their names. Well, neither Man nor Brother had children but Woman was with baby and her belly was full. Still, she was prepared to swim with Man, Brother and Brother's Woman to the new land. She wanted to give her baby a chance to live where the land would be kind to them. They spent the evening before they left preparing animal skins, which they greased on the inside with animal fat, then with the skin sewn up as tight as they could make it, they saved a last hole to breathe into just before they would be placed in the sea. They would use these to float across to the new land.' He winked at the boys, 'They were clever our ancestors, no?'

Both boys nodded.

'They sat around that last campfire with their tribe, saying goodbyes, and there was much crying and pleadings for them not to go but stay. Brother's Woman was very afraid and wanted to stay, but she fought with her fear and resolved to go wherever her man would go. The morning finally came, as mornings do, and it was a good day, the sun shone, the sky was blue and the sea, well the sea was calm and still. Everyone was hugged, then the four of them walked to the water's edge, turned and waved a farewell, before wading out to where the water was waist deep. They blew as much air as they could into the skins then tied shut the last hole, bending down they lay on the water, placed the skins under their chests and started to kick their legs to swim for that distant shore. The water was warm and they could see the sand passing slowly below them, between mounds of coral where shoals of small brightly coloured fish swam.

They had been swimming this way for a long time when Man looked back and saw that they were far from the shore; he could see his tribe lined along the beach waving when they saw him looking back. He waved one arm in reply then checked on his companions and saw that Woman was keeping pace with him, but Brother's Woman was trailing behind and that Brother had fallen back to stay with her. He called out to them,

'Keep up, keep up, we must stay together!'

Then he set his face once more on the shore ahead. The sea was very cold now and below them was only blackness. There was a breeze out there, causing small waves to slap into their faces, making it hard to breathe. They swam this way until the sun was high in the sky. Man was tired, but he could now make out individual trees on the shore ahead and this gave him new strength.

He smiled across at Woman to encourage her and she smiled back. Turning his head further back, he could make out the bobbing shapes of Brother and Brother's Woman a long way behind. He was about to turn back to face the shore when he saw to his horror that behind his brother and his woman were two large fins which were slicing through the water, moving closer and closer to them. He shouted a warning.'

'Brother, you are being followed, hurry, hurry, we

are nearly there.'

He saw Brother look over his shoulder, then saw him shouting to Brother's Woman. Soon spray could be seen flying into the air as they thrashed their legs to gain speed to escape from whatever was trailing behind them. Brother was terrified, thrashing his legs as fast as he could he moved across to swim alongside his woman. He saw that her eyes were wide with fear and her mouth gaped open as she gasped to breathe, her eyes were fixed straight ahead to the shore that was now so close.'

Deron looked down and saw that both of the boys were kneeling there with open mouths, trying to breathe for Brother's Woman.

'They were shoulder to shoulder and swimming for their lives when Brother's Woman suddenly disappeared from his side. He swirled around to see her, stationary and still laid across her float. She stretched out her hand to reach to him, her face in terror. He reached out to grasp her hand, but as their fingers touched she was dragged below the surface, and the last he saw of her was her hand still reaching out to him. He turned away and once more thrashed his legs to catch up with the now distant Man and Woman. Perhaps whatever had taken his woman would spare him. He was catching up with his brother when a massive force around his waist propelled him high above the water; held in enormous jaws he could see the surface of the water below and the dark body of the creature that held him. The palm of his hand brushed against the skin of the creature and his last thought was of how rough its skin was, before he was bitten through, falling in two halves into the sea.

Looking over his shoulder, Man saw his brother taken by the monster. He shouted encouragement to Woman to swim as fast as she could for the shore. The water beneath them turned light green once more, they could once again see sand and coral below. He expected to be attacked at any moment, forcing himself not to look behind, he carried on swimming until they came to the shallows and could stand. Even here, they did not stop, but surged up towards the beach as fast as they could, all the while the water seemed to drag them back, refusing to give them up to the land. When they were ankle-deep, they ran out of the sea to the top of the beach, where they collapsed to lie face down and gasping for air.

They lay there for a long time before they sat up and looked around them. The land looked much as the land they had left before the desert came. They stood and hand-in-hand walked away from the beach and into a forest. Now boys, the trees were not like the trees that surround us here. These trees were heavy with fruits to be plucked and eaten, as much as you could want.'

Rat held up his hand for Deron to stop his story.

'Fruits, what is fruits?'

'It is said that fruits are like berries, but juicier and as big as your fist, and that they taste wonderful to eat. It would be good if we had fruits here in these northern lands would it not boys?'

The boys nodded agreement.

'Well, they did eat their fill, and their stomachs ached that night. They were miserable to be in a strange land, with aching stomachs and with no tribe, who they missed terribly. But they did well in that new land and prospered together.'

Again, Rat halted the story.

'So, was this Woman the Mother of the Grovi?'

To himself, he was thinking how can just two humans become a race of people? Fathers would be fucking daughters and mothers fucking sons, and that was not right.

Deron was getting a little impatient at Rat's constant interruptions, but smiled at him and continued.

'No young Rat she was not, that is why I called her Woman. Eventually she gave birth to a daughter, and when this daughter was grown, it was she who became the Mother of the Grovi.'

Rat held up his hand again. 'But how, how could she become Mother of the Grovi, did she lie with her father, Man?'

Deron, swallowed and gently ground his teeth together.

'Perhaps, if you would shut up and let me finish, you would know how this came about. Enough now, if you stop me again you will not hear how this happened.'

He looked down sternly at Rat, who shamefacedly nodded and looked at the floor.

'Right, I will continue,' he shot a long hard look at Rat, then restarted his tale.

'The three humans lived in the forest, and roamed about it to pluck the fruits as they came into season. They travelled far and wide across the whole of that bountiful forest, until one day they reached the edge of the trees, there they looked out over a large lake that was surrounded by grass covered hills. They were happy to see so much water in one place, something that their daughter had never seen, being born in a forest far from the sea. Living by that lake, they found a small family of humans, different from themselves, but they were welcoming and invited them to sit by their fire. They stayed with that family for a long time, and the eldest son of that family came to be with the daughter of Man and Woman. A baby was born to the daughter, and in that moment the daughter became the Mother of the Grovi. So, you Brak, and all the other Grovi who ever lived came from that woman, who lived by a lake, in a land far to the south, and in a time that was beyond counting.'

He fell silent and looked at the boys, who looked back, not sure if the tale was done or not. Deron held out his hands with his palms out.

'There Rat, you have had what you asked for, now you know how the Grovi came to stand on the ground, but not how they came to the frozen north. That is for another time and takes many other stories to tell. So, go back to your hearth and leave me in peace tonight.'

He smiled and shooed them away with his hands. When they were sat once more by Brak's hearth, Brak asked Rat if he knew how the Salar came to be a tribe and Rat replied that he did not, but he would find out from his elders when he returned home. A long time later, Rat was sat with his own tribe's storyteller and asked him,

'Tell me, how did the Salar come to stand on this earth as a tribe, were we created by the Earth Mother, or did we have a human mother?'

The storyteller thought for while, then started on

his tale,

'Long, long ago in a land as far away as a place can be, there lived a small tribe of humans. This was a hot land, there was no ice or snow there, so these people wore no clothes and walked about as naked as babies.'

Rat smiled, made himself comfortable, and listened to the story being told once more.

18

THE LAST DAY

Rat lay remembering those times past for the remainder of the morning, until he saw by the fading of the light coming through the cave's entrance that the sun had passed its zenith. It was time to move. He went and retrieved the final bladder of water and the two squirrels, then returned to Brak. He tried to wake him, he shouted, he shook him, but nothing would bring him back. As he had done before, he used his fingers to lever Brak's jaws apart to insert the neck of the bladder and pour water into him, but the water filled his mouth, then ran over his lips to run down the side of his face and drip onto the cave floor.

Brak was breathing through his nose, so when Rat stopped pouring, the water just lay there cupped in his mouth. Rat turned Brak's head to allow the water to drain from his mouth, then sat back in despair. For his own sake, he gulped down half of the bladder's remaining contents and ate one of the squirrels. He should leave alone and soon, but he could not leave his friend behind like this. He lay down again by Brak's side and threw an arm over him. The light was starting to fade as the afternoon wore on when he felt Brak move. He looked at him and saw that his eyes were open and staring about wildly.

'Brak, it is Rat, speak to me man.'

Brak turned his head so that they lay there face to face.

'This Earth Mother of yours, would she take an unbeliever if you asked her?'

Rat replied in a voice that was shaky from the fear of losing his friend, but also at the thought of being left totally alone: to be the last man left in the north.

'Well yes, I have always prayed to her, telling her of you and your deeds. I would gladly ask for you.'

His voice became pleading.

'But you are not going to her yet, are you?'

'Does she forgive men, this god? I have killed many

men. I have been cruel when I could have been kind, and I have not shown mercy when mercy was right.'

He became agitated and with one hand grasped the fur on Rat's shoulder.

'Will my Culu be there, mmm? I would not want to live another life without her by my side. Say that I will find her there and I will gladly go to the Earth Mother, but if she is not then I will stay here to rot in this cave.'

'She will be there Brak, waiting for you with open arms, you will only have to step forwards to hold her again.'

Rat was panicking now, when he spoke there was desperation in his voice.

'But do not go yet friend, I need you here awhile, we can go to my home and sit by my hearth. Stay here Brak, I beg you, stay with me tonight.'

Brak stared into Rat's eyes, then seemed to come to a decision. He released his hold on Rat's shoulder, rolled onto his back, then took a deep breath and sighed. He lay there motionless with closed eyes.

Rat place his head on Brak's chest to feel him breathing. There was nothing, then his chest rose slightly and fell, nothing again, then the rise and fall; at least he is still alive thought Rat, there was still hope. Rat fussed around him, making sure that Brak was securely tucked into the furs, then lay by his side and once more threw his arm over his broad chest.

Slowly and steadily, the cave darkened through the afternoon until it was black night. Rat was half-asleep when Brak's body suddenly became rigid, then his arms and legs began to thrash about. Rat moved over him and laid across his chest, pulling Brak's arms tight against his body. He was bucked back and forth as Brak fought some unseen enemy, Rat wondered if he was once more fighting with the sea monster. Just when Rat was weakening and thought that he could restrain Brak no longer, Brak suddenly lay still. His body relaxed in Rat's arms, and a long sigh came from his lips, that stopped then restarted in a way that to Rat sounded almost like the name Culu.

'Brak, friend, you were having a nightmare, but you are alright now, it is me Rat, talk to me.'

The cave was silent. Rat lifted his head from Brak's chest, then taking one hand away from Brak's arm he placed it on his face. He gently traced his fingers over his eyes and found that they were open, but did not close when Rat's fingers brushed against them. He choked back a sob and lowered his head back down onto Brak's chest. With his arms wrapped around his friend for one last time, he wept in the darkness. After the tears had stopped and were drying on his face, he sat up. The silence and total darkness in the cave was suffocating him, he felt as if he was floating alone in a shapeless void that did not belong on the earth and was outside of time and space. If he allowed this to continue any longer he felt that he would go mad with fear.

Hurriedly, he rummaged in the sacks and found the fire-stones and the candles, but his hands were shaking so much that he could not make a spark that would catch. He forced himself, terrified as he was, to strike the stones the way he had done so many times before, the way he was first shown how to make fire as a child. Eventually, he successfully lit the first one and the dark retreated away from him. He used the first candle to light three more and placed the four candles at Brak's head, sides and feet, then he leaned over Brak and closed his eyelids. He sat and looked at his friend's body lying there, with his lips drawn slightly back and up it seemed as if he was smiling as he passed; in his left hand was the red coral-bead necklace that Culu had worn. He looked no different now than he had in life, and could at any moment open his eyes and gruffly demand to know why Rat was staring at him.

While he still had light, Rat found his shaman's black robe and pulled it around him, then kneeling at Brak's feet he put on his mask and started to chant. The sounds he made were ancient, from longer ago than any could remember, passed down countless times from shaman to shaman. The meanings had been lost long ago, but the form of the keening remained unchanged. After almost completing the full cycle of chants he fell silent, then started a final wail that began with a deep sound low in his chest, so quiet it was almost below the level of hearing, that continued to build in volume and rise in pitch until it climaxed with his head thrown back, teeth bared in a snarl and with his arms thrown behind him. A wail so loud and fierce that the small flames danced about as if trying escape from their candles, before settling to be still once more when finally the cry died in his throat as a choked sob. He collapsed onto the floor, invisible beneath the mask and the gathered folds of the black robe. When he had recovered he knelt once more and started to pray.

'Earth Mother, I beseech you to take my fried Brak to your world and reunite him with his woman, Culu. He was a good man, a great warrior and chief. He was also a good friend to me, never cruel, always kind. I would not be your shaman if it were not for the care that Brak gave me when we were young. Please see that my tribe, the Salar, are kept safe in the south and that Brak's tribe also prosper forever in this world.'

He tried to control his breathing before continuing.

'I hope that you can see me in this cave alone, with no human but me left in the north. I need your motherly love to save me and see that I live to see spring return to the valleys. I am coming now to visit your world, but I am not ready yet to stay. I ask that you allow me to come, then if you will, let me return to this place after and continue living until I am ready to pass.'

When he had finished he looked and saw that the candles would soon go out. He had no more candles and he could not, would not, stay here when the darkness returned to envelop him. He took up a bag and quickly selected some berries and herbs that would temporarily release him from this place. When, as a boy, Sabal was training him to be a shaman, he had told him that he must never, ever, place these berries directly into his mouth, they were far too dangerous.

'Do you hear me boy? You must remember this, for your life's sake, always heat these berries first in water and then drink the liquid, never swallow them or you will risk your death.'

Then Sabal slapped the boy so hard across his face that it left a red imprint of his hand behind.

'Remember!'

Rat never forgot the warning, but now he had no choice, this was his only escape from the terror in the dark cave. One candle went out, then another. In the half darkness, Rat felt the eyes of the ancient beast behind him watching, and he was terrified that the corpse in front of him might come back to life in the dark, sit up and call out to him. He took a handful of the berries and herbs and placed them in his mouth, then he filled his mouth with water and chewed. The taste was dreadfully bitter, but he fought back the urge to retch, crushing the herbs and berries between his teeth, before swallowing the juice, then spitting out the pulp onto the floor.

He lay down at Brak's feet and, with a final glance at the skeleton at the back of the cave, closed his eyes. The last two candles sputtered out and the darkness returned. He felt the fear grip him, but then he relaxed and felt himself rising up, suddenly finding himself flying as a sea-eagle high above the ridge. Looking down, he could see in the moonlight the dark shape of a snow leopard lying on the snow-covered roof of the cave, yawning as its tail twitched backwards and forwards. As he watched, the leopard stood, walked to be above the cave mouth, then leapt down to land by Roden's body. It looked down on the corpse, sniffed it, then turned away and loped off across the flat ground before disappearing down into the forest-covered slope below the ridge.

He continued to fly in a climbing circle above the two valleys. Far below, he saw Brak's long-house, the snow-covered roof shining brightly in the moonlight, the long shadow of the tusk pointing towards the beach where the huddle of standing stones were keeping guard. He turned and flew over his own valley, where he could see the tight cluster of round-houses by the ribbon of the river as it shimmered silver on its way down to the sea. He felt ecstatically happy as he flew higher and higher, then suddenly he banked over in a wide arc across the sky, the silhouette of the eagle flashed across the face of the moon before levelling out to head south, searching for his two tribes.

SECRETS

Ramsay could tell by the pelvic girdle of the skeleton that it was a man, who, judging by the heavy bones, would have been powerfully built. Resting across the finger bones of his left hand was a beautiful red coral-bead necklace. He was quite certain, even after only three years of studying his snow-depth readings, that the cave entrance must have been covered for thousands of years and, as the bones had never been disturbed, either by man or by animals, he was the first to see this man's remains since he had died here so long ago. His overriding feeling was that he was intruding here, there was a chapel-like stillness in this place that should not be disturbed. His gaze was drawn to the eye-sockets, so large in the skull, staring back at him, as if commanding him to leave.

He quickly pulled out his phone, and standing as high as he could, took a picture. As the flash of the camera lit the skeleton, he took in an involuntary half-breath from the guilt of bringing the banal technology of the twenty-first century into such an ancient scene. He chided himself for being so fanciful, then turned and dropped on all fours again to return once more to the skeleton at the back of the cave. Once there, he lifted the camera up to take a photograph of the imposing skeleton of the beast, and again in the harsh flash took the sudden intake of breath and the feeling that he should leave at once. He could feel the small hairs on the back of his neck prickle in fear and, slightly dazzled by the flash, he shot a glance over his shoulder to the cave-mouth to check that the way was still open and he was not entombed here with these two dead creatures. He stood up and crashed the top of his head against the roof of the cave, stunned for a moment, he turned, then staggered to the cave entrance and out once more into the bright sunlight and the cold fresh air.

He regained his breath and his composure, then set about walling up the cave-mouth with snow, he wanted there to be no trace of the cave visible after he left. He had decided that he would not mention this place to anyone, he knew what would happen if he did: the bones of both skeletons would be hauled off and mounted in display cabinets in some museum, to be gawped at through glass walls by bored parents and their children. When he was satisfied that the cave-mouth was completely covered over, he went and waited to be picked up by the helicopter. It was some hours later, in the coach travelling from the airport to the hotel, that one of the film-crew, who were all in high spirits after getting the shots that they had been hoping for, pointed to Ramsay's forehead and asked him why blood was running down from his hair. He put up a hand and felt the wetness, before making an excuse that he had stumbled and struck his head on a rock. It was then that he realised that he had left behind some of his blood on the roof of that sealed dark tomb.

He never did tell anyone about the cave. A bachelor, he had no wife to confide in, and there was no one else in his life so close that he would risk telling them. The closest that he came was one night, after drinking a little too much whisky with a colleague who was an paleontologist, when he pulled his phone from his jacket-pocket and showed him the photograph of the large skeleton lying at the back of the cave. The man was impressed.

'Wow, Alan, that's a Cave Bear, they've been extinct for thousands of years, where did you take this?'

But Ramsay just smiled, said nothing and returned the phone to his pocket. Three years after he had found the cave he presented his research paper at a climate-change conference, but received only a smattering of applause in recognition for all of his hard work There was no invitation from a large prestigious university, so he stayed where he was until he at last retired. Often, late at night as he sat alone in his study, he would look at the two photographs and remember the cave, hoping that the entrance continued to be hidden by snow. Still in darkness, still keeping its secrets.

ABOUT THE AUTHOR

The author has held many positions: working in a steel-mill, in an oil-refinery, driving locomotives and working on oil-rigs in the North Sea. He returned onshore to work on several major construction projects, then went offshore again to work on gas-rigs in the Irish Sea. Latterly, he took the position as a manager in a university. He has a Masters Degree and gained professional Chartered status. For recreation, the author is a qualified scuba diver, studied karate, and at various times went paragliding, sailing, windsurfing and surfing. When not writing he also plays guitar, badly. He lives in a small cottage by an English seashore, with a very large Russian Black Terrier called Molly.

Printed in Great Britain
by Amazon.co.uk, Ltd.,
Marston Gate.

8142269R00212